THE
FATAL
SCROLL

A Herculaneum Mystery

THE
FATAL
SCROLL

ERIC SIBLIN

Published by ECW Press
665 Gerrard Street East
Toronto, Ontario, Canada M4M 1Y2
416-694-3348 / info@ecwpress.com

Cover design: David Drummond
Cover image: iStock

LIBRARY AND ARCHIVES CANADA CATALOGUING IN PUBLICATION

Title: The fatal scroll / Eric Siblin.

Names: Siblin, Eric, author.

Description: Series statement: A Herculaneum mystery ; 1

Identifiers: Canadiana (print) 20250140349 | Canadiana (ebook) 20250140365

ISBN 978-1-77041-840-0 (softcover)
ISBN 978-1-77852-416-5 (ePub)
ISBN 978-1-77852-417-2 (PDF)

Subjects: LCGFT: Novels. | LCGFT: Detective and mystery fiction.

Classification: LCC PS8637.I2345 F38 2025 | DDC C813/.6—dc23

This book is funded in part by the Government of Canada. *Ce livre est financé en partie par le gouvernement du Canada.* We acknowledge the support of the Canada Council for the Arts. *Nous remercions le Conseil des arts du Canada de son soutien.* We would like to acknowledge the funding support of the Ontario Arts Council (OAC) and the Government of Ontario for their support. We also acknowledge the support of the Government of Ontario through the Ontario Book Publishing Tax Credit, and through Ontario Creates.

PRINTED AND BOUND IN CANADA

PRINTING: MARQUIS   5 4 3 2 1

For a wrongdoer to be undetected is difficult; and for him to have confidence that his concealment will continue is impossible.

— EPICURUS (341–270 BC)

1

PAPYRUS

It was a misshapen object, roughly the size of an eggplant, badly charred and flaking black powder, that led Marcus Sinclair to southern Italy.

The item in question was a papyrus scroll — an ancient book — burnt to high hell in a volcanic eruption and buried in mud and ash for seventeen centuries. Marcus inherited the scroll from his uncle, an antiquities dealer with a multimillion-dollar estate that included artifacts from long-vanished empires. Gerald Sinclair, who died at the age of ninety-two, had himself been something of a relic, doing most of his business in an era which had little patience for concerns like record-keeping and transparency. "Make things happen," he liked to say. "Ask questions later."

It didn't take much research online to confirm the scroll's origins, which Gerald described in a post-mortem letter to his nephew as a "papyrus from the ancient Roman town of Herculaneum." Marcus taught European history at a community college, but the name *Herculaneum* rang only a distant bell. Online, he was astonished to learn that Herculaneum was one of the most spectacular discoveries in archaeological history — the largest haul of ancient statues ever found in one place, along with mosaics and wall paintings of exquisite beauty. It also contained the only library to have survived the ancient classical world.

Like its famous neighbour, Pompeii, Herculaneum was snuffed out of existence by the eruption of Mount Vesuvius in AD 79. The town's natural materials, from wooden doors to olive pits, were carbonized — burnt, but not destroyed — by the superheated gasses of the volcano. Among the artifacts so transformed were papyrus scrolls. Some of those blackened scrolls were successfully opened and deciphered, most of them consisting of ancient philosophy. But several hundred scrolls were too damaged to be unrolled and read.

In the letter to Marcus, Gerald explained how the scroll had ended up in his possession. He had procured it for a client "through the usual channels — common at the time, if not entirely legal — no questions asked, no paperwork," but "developed a curious affection" for the scroll, choosing to keep it for himself, telling the client that his shadowy connections had failed to secure it. "Whoever can unlock the Herculaneum scrolls will not only go down in history but also make themselves quite rich."

Gerald's legacy, meanwhile, had made Marcus quite rich. Part of the inheritance was Gerald's luxury condo — Marcus never imagined he'd move into his uncle's place on Hazelton Row in Toronto's upmarket Yorkville. It was a far cry from his apartment in the Parkdale area, where pawn shops, bars, and beggars were fighting a rear-guard action against gentrification. Once he began spending time in a condo outfitted with central air-conditioning, a jetted tub, a walk-in closet, and still pleasantly scented with Gerald's pipe tobacco, Marcus felt a magnetic emotional pull. He started sleeping in that strangely comforting space decorated with vases, pillars, mosaics, and various objects made of bronze, terracotta, and marble.

One afternoon, some two months after Gerald's death, his uncle's phone rang, the landline Marcus had been meaning to disconnect. He'd been in no rush to do so, as if erasing those familiar seven digits would be a final wrenching break with the past. The landline only rang with telemarketing calls. He reluctantly picked up the receiver, expecting more of the same. But the voice at the other end belonged to Laszlo Kacsmarik, an old pal of Gerald's.

"Young Sinclair!" Laszlo said in his stubbornly Hungarian English. "The professor!"

"No longer. Semi-retired now. At least once I finish marking this last mountain of essays. It's painful, but not for much longer. Gerald left me a nice inheritance."

"I know. That's why I'm calling you. Your uncle might have remembered his old Magyar friend." A chuckle segued into a cough.

Laszlo had been something of a fixer for Gerald. Marcus remembered him as a handyman for the family. He was now an art restorer.

"I have something to tell you," Laszlo said. "To show you."

"Really? What's this about?"

"About a papyrus. An old papyrus scroll."

Another scroll?

"I want to discuss this in person," Laszlo said. "Come to my studio. Anytime. I'm almost always here."

An ambulance sounded somewhere outside, its siren making long, shrill loops. Marcus mouthed a short prayer, six words in Hebrew, a superstitious habit he'd picked up from Gerald, who did the same thing whenever an ambulance passed by. His uncle had never been a religious man but was a Holocaust survivor who'd escaped Nazi Europe. Intoning a few sacred words when an ambulance raced by was a method of sending good luck to someone who needed it.

After the phone call, Marcus went into Gerald's bedroom, where he'd first laid eyes on the scroll. He'd fished it out of a Roman amphora, as per the instructions in his uncle's letter. The two-handled jug stood about two feet high, decorated with a black warrior figure slaying some mythological beast. It was covered by a plastic lid and surmounted with a sleek reading lamp of Scandinavian design — a cheeky use of an ancient artifact, in keeping with Gerald's maverick way of doing things.

Marcus removed the lamp and plastic lid from the amphora, checking that the papyrus was still there, swaddled in thick cotton, encased in a Teflon bag and placed in a vacuum-sealed container. It weighed next to nothing. A black box that had crashed and burned. Sealed with the kiss of Vesuvius.

LASZLO'S STUDIO WAS ON QUEEN STREET WEST, above a picture-framing shop called Hang Ups. Marcus climbed the stairs, taking them two at a time. He hadn't played tennis lately so was happy to have a short burst of activity. Once inside, he found Laszlo looking not so different from when Marcus last saw him, about seven years earlier, at Gerald's eighty-fifth birthday dinner. Laszlo was still a thin man, a wispy moustache and goatee giving him a youthful appearance that camouflaged his age.

"Your shop looks great," Marcus said.

Laszlo pulled a handkerchief out of his jacket pocket to wipe his eyes and nose. "At this point," he said, "it's more a work of love than anything else."

"How do you mean?"

"Art restoration is not what it was. Everything is digital now. I'm an old craftsman. Not walking with the times. But I'm still active. My hands do not shake. Not a bit." He fluttered his two hands as if they were wings and left them to sit motionless in the air, mottled, liver-spotted, bent out of shape. "But I didn't bring you here to see my beautiful hands. Come, take a look."

He led Marcus to the back of the dimly lit workshop.

"I know you were supposed to inherit the papyrus, Marcus. I guess Gerald told you about the work I did on it?"

"What work? He didn't mention anything about your work. He just left me a letter saying it was from Herculaneum and wishing me luck figuring it out."

"Classic Gerald. Tough as marble, that man."

Marcus considered the image. Gerald had been smooth. Old world. High end. Resistant to cracking. But he did crack and break, weakening as everyone does in the end. And on a bathroom floor in fact made of marble, requiring that final hospitalization. Marcus could almost feel the hard landing, old bones on old marble. Was that the function of older relatives: role models, cautionary tales for your own demise? What would his own inevitable fall look like?

Marcus said, "What sort of work did you do?"

"He brought me the scroll and wanted to know how we might unroll it," Laszlo said. "I tried. Nothing worked. I mean, how in paradise can that scroll be restored to its normal condition? There are layers and layers in there, fused together, and every layer is extremely brittle. It's impossible . . . well, almost impossible."

From outside on Queen Street came the jarring screech of a passing streetcar.

Laszlo said, "You know the history of these scrolls, how they tried to unroll them?"

"I know some of it. I know it hasn't been easy."

"It's been torture. When they were discovered in 1750 or so, the King of Naples appointed a painter to open them. The painter cut the scrolls vertically in half with a knife, trying to show some writing to impress the king. He came up with bits of text, but in the process butchered many scrolls."

"I guess he didn't get his hands on Gerald's scroll," Marcus said.

"Luckily not, but many others were destroyed. The king brought in various experts but, you know, experts from *three hundred years ago*.

One of them, a prince who was also an alchemist, brewed a potion of mercury and other chemicals. Soaked a papyrus in this concoction. Guess what happened? It dissolved into pulp! Then a famous chemist tried with some sort of vegetable gas. More failure. More scrolls destroyed. Another scroll was placed under a glass bell to loosen the layers, but the heat from the sun bleached the writing so that no one could read it. Nothing worked. Nothing except this."

Laszlo gestured to a wood-framed contraption that brought to mind a guillotine or, less grimly, a Pilates contraption. "It's a sort of traction machine to unroll the Herculaneum scrolls."

"Wow," Marcus said. "I know about this thing. It was invented by a priest, right?"

"Father Antonio Piaggio, from the Vatican. He specialized in illuminated manuscripts. Hero of the story."

"I assume this isn't his original machine? So I'm guessing you built this yourself?"

"With my own hands!"

Silky threads dangled from the top of the machine, designed, Laszlo explained, to be fastened to the outer leaf of a papyrus scroll. "Eighteenth-century technology," he said. "Piaggio used these sorts of threads, leather straps, steel pins, screws, and sheep intestines, which were glued to the exposed end of a papyrus scroll. That was a challenge. I needed an adhesive that was strong enough to pull the papyrus but not tear it. I thought I could find a synthetic equivalent, but nothing worked very well. It was hard to improve upon Piaggio's original invention. This could almost be one of his machines from the 1700s. With one exception. I could not find any sheep gut from the eighteenth century. Used some tripe I got in Chinatown."

Laszlo fiddled with a screw on the machine. "The scroll would be attached here to a pulley by thread. These keys here — he grazed his hand across a row of pegs like those used to tune a violin — are slowly turned so that the layers of the scroll can be separated and raised."

Marcus said, "This is incredible. I can't believe you managed to build this thing."

"Not bad for an old-timer, eh? Not me. I mean the scroll." Laszlo's laugh morphed into a cough, the sandpaper timbre of a longtime smoker.

"I had no idea! Gerald's letter to me suggested he never even tried to get the scroll unrolled."

"Maybe he wrote his letter before we got this idea," Laszlo said. "Anyway, I unrolled about half an inch a day. For about a month. Then the scroll broke."

"It broke?"

"It tore. I could not unroll any more. Nobody can, because it's all fused together in one chunk. So I gave the papyrus back to Gerald. Now I'm stuck with this." He nodded at the traction machine. "But I will give you what I unrolled and cut off. That's why I called."

Laszlo removed a plastic tarp from a nearby worktable. It held a blackened page enclosed in a metal frame, a sheet of papyrus glued to a stiff board. It was a segment of Gerald's scroll, bearing dark letters on a dark background.

"Father Piaggio worked the same way," Laszlo said. "Whenever he'd unrolled a sizable section from a papyrus, say half a metre, he'd cut it off and glue it to a sheet of cardboard."

"It's in Latin," Marcus said.

"It is. Not that I can make very much sense of it. Also, some of the words are missing. The machine is not perfect, it destroys some of the material while it unrolls." He handed Marcus a sheet of typescript paper. "This is the writing, best as I can make out."

Marcus scanned the page, which began, *Epist . . . ollectae Luci . . . Cal . . . Pis . . . Caeson . . . .*

He had only a passing familiarity with Latin. Struggling with the text, which was broken by gaps, he wished he'd taken more than that one undergraduate Latin course ages ago. What appeared to be a hodge-podge of foreign words was mostly unintelligible to him.

Ca . . . Imp . . . Pisoni Sal . . . D.
Si vales bene est. Quid agit illa villa delicat . . .
. . . Inimicis nunc superatis Munda . . . Romam . . .
Scio te . . . obligandi me avide amplecti . . .
in testamento . . . heredem . . . filium Aegypto . . . sic iube . . .

"What does this mean?"

"Who knows?" Laszlo said. "I couldn't tell you. But it seems Gerald wanted you to figure it out."

Marcus thought of Gerald's letter, the part where he urged his nephew to "follow the trail of the papyrus." The trail had come to an abrupt end on the Piaggio machine. All that remained was a jumble of truncated letters in a dead language. And a burnt-out scroll that might as well still be buried in lava, mud, and ash.

2

HERCULANEUM

A few months passed while Marcus was busy with teaching, grading, and settling Gerald's estate. He also moved out of his apartment, which meant discarding needless stuff that had long cluttered the space. What he couldn't purge, he packed, filed, and carted into Gerald's storage locker. He was adept at compartmentalizing. There were compartments in his head containing family turmoil, work frustrations, spiritual longings, health concerns, and past relationships. Containers within containers that held a lifetime of regrets, fears, and half-baked hopes. Change what you can change, so said Stoicism. Or more to the point: don't change what you're not up to changing. Just store it in a compartment. Drift. Accept. Drift some more.

Meanwhile, the little papyrus scroll loomed large in his imagination. The best he could figure out from the text, using online translation tools, was a smattering of phrases like *enemies now overcome . . . Rome . . .* and *eagerly embrace me to oblige* and *Egypt.* Laszlo had been on the right track: the rest of the scroll would have to somehow be opened.

From time to time, Marcus would search online for ideas on how to unroll it. But there were no obvious solutions. Then he learned that an academic conference about the Herculaneum scrolls was to take place the following month in Italy. The timing of the conference was so convenient that he felt obliged, fated even, to register. The teaching semester was behind him. And in any case, an inheritance north of five million dollars enabled Marcus to quit a job he'd liked less and less with every passing year.

"You sure you want to do this?" said one of his teaching colleagues.

"I'm sure," said Marcus.

She shook her head skeptically. "What will you do?"

"I'm not sure. I may have to take up hedonism."

She laughed. "You're too old to master new skills."

Maybe so. But all his loose ends were tied up, and the rest of his life stretched out before him like an ocean's vast horizon. At age fifty-one, single with no children, he was suddenly, prematurely, retired, in upgraded material circumstances. But the good fortune made him feel as if he had about as much purpose as a piece of driftwood. He wanted to do something, for once in his life. Gerald's scroll became that something. So in the final days of July, he caught an evening flight to Rome followed by an afternoon train to Naples. Packed in his hard-shell carry-on, nestled in its own form-fitting case built by Laszlo, was an eggplant-sized papyrus scroll.

THE TOWN OF HERCULANEUM, *Ercolano* in Italian, according to the guidebook on his phone, was a spot where tourists admired the archae-ological site and got out of town before the sun dipped over the ruins. Or before Mount Vesuvius, less than eight kilometres away, once again released its pent-up fury. But unlike most who visited the place,

Marcus checked into the Hotel Greco, a pink-toned building with palatial aspirations. It was surrounded by a sprawling garden filled with crumbling gazebos, fountains, and statues — a ruin in and of itself. An apt venue for the Sixth Biennial Conference of the Friends of Herculaneum.

Ercolano itself appeared sleepy and provincial. It was a short walk along a narrow street to the only recommended restaurant, the Rosso Vesuvio, equal parts authentic and touristic, featuring checkered tablecloths, a beige tiled floor, and whitewashed walls hung with paintings of Mount Vesuvius. One of Europe's most devastating natural disasters airbrushed for tourists. Marcus thought of fiery lava, choking clouds of ash, and a furnace blast of heat that asphyxiated all living creatures.

A waiter snapped him out of his trance: "May I help you?"

He was soon seated at a table adjacent to a portly, baby-faced man in his forties who was wearing a Seattle Mariners baseball cap and a T-shirt that proclaimed *Good Data Is Hard to Find*. The man's plate was filled with perfectly grilled calamari, golden at the edges, flaked with herbs, and anointed with oil. Also on the table was a glass of red wine, a basket of crusty bread, and the Herculaneum conference program.

Marcus said, "I see you're also here for the conference?"

"I am! You as well?"

His name was Trevor Ballard, and he was a software engineer with Google.

"I'm new to all this Herculaneum stuff," Ballard said.

"I know the feeling. But why's Google interested?"

"It's not Google; it's me. Google allows its managers to spend one day a week on a non-work-related issue. They call it the twenty percent rule. What you do doesn't even have to be potentially money-making."

"Really? Nice work if you can get it."

Trevor Ballard said, "It happens a lot in tech. That's how 3M invented the Post-it Note. I'm making Herculaneum my twenty percent. The papyrus scrolls: there has to be some digital way to unroll and decipher them. I thought I could offer some ideas. I'm not sure the technology is quite there yet. But things are moving fast in this area, and the papyrus scholars aren't up to speed with all the new stuff that's happening in tech."

A waiter appeared, and Marcus ordered a salad and a margherita pizza. No wine. If only alcohol had the soporific effect on him that it had on everyone else he knew! Instead, booze kept him awake for many sheep-counting hours. At least he didn't have to stress anymore about getting to work in the morning. Those days, thanks to Gerald, were over.

"What brings you here?"

"I don't really have any business being here," Marcus said. "Not even twenty percent business."

He held back on mentioning his scroll. "I'm a community college history teacher. Or used to be. I took early retirement. Came into an inheritance."

"Sweet."

"Looking for something to fill my days now. I stumbled onto this conference online, did a bunch of reading on the subject. It's mostly the philosophy I find interesting."

"The Epicureans, right?"

"And their rivals, the Stoics."

"Everyone's claiming to be a Stoic in Silicon Valley these days," Ballard said.

"I read something about that. Amazing how in-depth these philosophies were. Super specific about how to live life. How to arrange your finances, your love life, your morality, you name it — happiness, friendship, politics, physics, the gods, death. It's all there."

"Don't you have Siri for that?"

The waiter brought a steaming plate of spaghetti with clams for Ballard and the pizza for Marcus. An hour passed during which

Ballard drank more wine, and their conversation meandered pleasantly across a range of topics: the similarity between the pizza oven's temperature and that of a volcanic eruption; the erotic collection of antiquities still kept under lock and key in the Naples museum; the U.S. air force strafing of Vesuvius in 1944, which triggered its most recent eruption.

They soon headed back to the hotel along Corso Resina, slightly late for the "meet and greet" that was kicking off the conference. Marcus, who grew restless after sitting for any length of time, felt like stretching his strong legs and sprinting ahead. But Ballard had the slow gait of a man carrying extra bulk. They walked along the side of the road, the sky darkening, until they were back at the Hotel Greco. At a registration table in the hotel garden, they were given laminated name tags that depicted a leaping pig.

"What's with the little piggies?" Ballard asked.

"Symbol of Epicureanism," Marcus said.

"Why?"

"Not sure, but I think it was a slur way back when against the Epicureans for believing in pleasure above all else. Pigs at the trough?"

A few dozen people gathered in the garden, sipping from plastic cups of wine. How déclassé, Marcus thought; no better than History department wine and cheese events.

"Is Google going to rescue us?"

The question was posed by Olivier Auger, a renowned French papyrologist whose name Marcus recognized from his research.

"What do you need to be rescued from?" Ballard asked.

"I personally have no need to be rescued. But the Herculaneum archaeological site does. And some people are wondering why Google is here."

"I'm here to learn," Ballard said.

"Ah, join our little club. *Bienvenue!*"

They raised their plastic cups of wine.

Here's a man, an academic star, Marcus thought, whose tools of the trade consist of a magnifying glass, a pencil, and a few dictionaries. Pure scholarship. If Marcus had mustered the discipline and ambition to finish his Ph.D., he imagined he'd be some version of that man. Or at least a long-haired version. Auger was bald as Michel Foucault.

"So what's it like," Marcus asked, "being a papyrologist?"

"It's difficult work." Auger swirled the wine around in his cup. "But it's, we can say, formidable when you're working on a text written two thousand years ago. You have to be careful not to even breathe too hard so the moisture you exhale doesn't damage the papyrus. And there it is. It's right in front of you, touching your nose. So you start figuring it out, letter by letter, and transcribe it for the first time. It is a grand puzzle. With missing pieces. *Un mystère.* I am like a detective."

"It seems super time-consuming," Ballard said. "Is there not some technology that could speed up the detective work?"

"I'm not pressed. These papyri can teach many things. It cannot be rushed." He sipped more wine, looking every inch a man happy to take his time in life.

"Also," piped in a German professor who'd joined them, "we don't know what masterpieces are still buried underground. Only a tiny percentage of the Villa dei Papiri, where the scrolls were discovered, has been excavated. The real story is what other books, possible masterpieces, have not yet been discovered."

"I'll drink to that," Auger said. "To the health of all those papyri taking a siesta underground."

Marcus glanced around the candlelit garden. Conference attendees formed little scrums of animated conversation fuelled by Neapolitan hors d'oeuvres and wine from the foothills of Vesuvius. The sort of schmoozefest he normally stayed away from, given the choice. He was not good at socializing beyond one-on-one chats. And he was now reminded of being a kid in a schoolyard during recess and watching his classmates busy at play, fascinated by the spectacle, and having to remind his young self that he should also be playing.

Not much had changed. With Ballard and Auger deep in conversation, Marcus stepped away and walked around the garden, peering at name tags. He recognized the name of another star papyrologist. David Brill, a tall reed of a man with thick glasses and angular features, was holding forth in a British accent, several people hanging on his every word.

"If I ever find the time, I will go back to Socrates," Brill was saying. "How was it that being a philosopher in the Athens of his time was such a dangerous line of work?"

Marcus kept moving. How to separate the arcana at the conference from the useful information? It was like sifting through sand and dirt on an archaeological dig. How to figure out who might help unroll and decipher Gerald's scroll? Auger was one option. Yet Ballard was the obvious candidate. And Google. If anyone could scroll through a scroll and make sense of it . . .

He'd circled back to Ballard and Auger, who were now chatting with two younger papyrologists, a German and an Italian. Auger, his face flushed with wine, explained how he was working on a remarkable Herculaneum scroll that had been unrolled long ago but had never been properly edited. "I have great hopes of completing the translation because it's a short text. I don't want to wait another twenty-five years to finish like my last work."

"What is the scroll?" Ballard asked.

"The papyrus is important and poetic. By the Epicurean philosopher Philodemus. Titled 'On Tranquility.' It's a *bijou*, a jewel."

Marcus looked at Auger. In the glow of nearby candlelight, his creased face seemed to radiate serenity. He asked the French scholar whether he considered himself an Epicurean.

"Yes, *absolument*," he replied. "And it has helped me. A few years ago, I had stomach cancer surgery. The situation was deplorable."

His small audience drew closer and listened intently.

"It was very grave. I didn't know whether I would survive. I did, evidently. But before the surgery, I had a very philosophical mentality and told myself, to quote Epicurus: death is nothing."

Nothing? So far as Marcus could see, *nothing* — that's to say oblivion — was precisely the problem.

"I have made close friends," Auger continued. "I have had a good career, I know what it is like to have great love. I had tranquility. And it helped. What we Epicureans call *ataraxia*."

"*Ataraxia*," Ballard repeated. "There should be an app for that."

"Epicureanism," Auger said. "The only app you will ever need."

A stocky man, unshaven, with heavily tattooed arms, had joined their circle of conversation. He introduced himself as Spiros Dima, an archaeologist working at the Herculaneum ruins, and soon started quizzing Ballard about Google.

Ballard was evasive about Google's interest in Herculaneum. Instead, he asked the man, "Why aren't they excavating at the Villa dei Papiri, where the library is? Where the scrolls were found? I mean, like ninety-nine percent of the Villa is still underground, no?"

"They'll never restart digging at the Villa," the archaeologist replied. "Nor should they."

"That would be unfortunate," said the German. "There is no other spot on the planet where there's such a strong likelihood of finding ancient books that have been lost to history."

"There aren't many other places," countered the archaeologist, "where you can stroll through a two-thousand-year-old city like this. And I should know — I'm half Greek. Herculaneum and Pompeii, that's it. And if they restart excavations at the Villa, it will all go to shit! The Italians don't have the resources to maintain Herculaneum. It's crumbling as we speak. Rain, pollution, landslides, theft, two hundred and fifty thousand tourists marching through every year. You know how many custodians the site has a budget for today? Two! If we start digging for your imagined books, the ruins will take a massive hit, suffer more damage, and further deplete the small budget for the site. Remember: it's fucking expensive to dig. They'll never do it. Not in your lifetime. They can't."

The tattoos on his muscular arms spoke to his line of work: a Doric column, a shovel, a vase, a smattering of Greek and Latin words.

"The site needs emergency first aid. It's falling apart," he continued. "Falling chunks of plaster. Frescoes flaking off. It's a conservation crisis. Towns like Herculaneum are rarer than your papyrus rolls."

"Understood," Ballard said, catching Marcus's eye, acknowledging that the archaeologist was more than a little inebriated. "But the scrolls, if they're down there, are also in trouble. Apparently, there's the threat of flooding and subterranean water seepage. Or another earthquake. Not to mention the volcano. If we don't . . ."

"You imagine Google can just waltz in here and save the day," said the archaeologist. "You people don't know your ass from your elbow. I'm half American, so I can say this without prejudice. I'm the one in the trenches. Dirt. Dust. Tufa, volcanic mud hard as cement. The polluted air. The dogs. The syringes of addicts. The pigeons and their shit. If you think software can solve anything here, well, just stick around."

3

NAPLES

Over the next three days, Marcus and Ballard sat through long lectures about papyrus scrolls. They buttonholed experts, toured the ruins of Herculaneum, hiked Mount Vesuvius, explored Naples, and feasted on exquisite meals. Totally bitten, as Ballard phrased it, with the Herculaneum bug. Now they sat at a sidewalk table drinking espresso at the Caffè Gambrinus, comparing notes about the conference, which had ended the previous day. They had one more item on their agenda. Professor David Brill had invited a few of the non-academics attending the conference to visit the "Officina," where the Herculaneum scrolls — those that had been excavated — were stored and studied.

"Beautiful day," Marcus said.

"Not as beautiful as seeing a two-thousand-year-old papyrus in the flesh," Ballard said.

"Yeah, but you don't need a high-powered microscope for Naples."

"Speak for yourself."

Across the street stood the sprawling pink-and-grey Royal Palace of Naples. It rubbed shoulders with the San Carlo opera house, built in 1737, the oldest in Europe. Between the café and the palace lay the Piazza del Plebiscito, a vast square with a Pantheon-style church, equestrian statues, and in the far distance, beyond the glittering Bay of Naples, Mount Vesuvius.

"Anyway," Marcus said, "a microscope won't do much good for a scroll that hasn't been unrolled."

"True," Ballard said. "Which is why I'm here."

Marcus had been weighing the pros and cons of sharing his secret about Gerald's scroll. Ballard had won his confidence. No one he'd met during the conference seemed more capable of finding a way to decipher the thing. The old method — the Piaggio machine — took forever and did not work on the vast majority of Herculaneum scrolls because of how damaged they were. Gerald's scroll was a case in point: Laszlo was adamant that he'd done all he could using the Piaggio machine without further mutilating the scroll.

Marcus said, "Can I confide in you about something?"

"Confide away. What happens in Naples stays . . ."

"I have a scroll."

"What?"

"From Herculaneum. Still rolled. Or mostly. Not sure what to do with it."

"Are you serious? Why haven't you mentioned this till now?"

Marcus felt a spasm of guilt. The longer he went without telling the truth about something, the harder it was to come clean.

"I inherited it from my uncle. It's the reason I'm here. I'm not sure how he got it. I wanted to be discreet."

"Understood. Wow! Do you have it with you here?"

"Yes."

"Amazing! And what are you planning to do with it?"

"I'd like to unroll it. Read it. If that's at all possible."

Marcus looked up to see Professor Brill approaching with his wide-brimmed straw hat and blue knapsack. Two amateur enthusiasts from the conference tagged along: a retired British school teacher and a hedge-fund manager from Connecticut who had brought along his bored teenage son.

"It's possible," Ballard said. "And right in my wheelhouse."

"To be continued," Marcus said, nodding in Brill's direction.

"There's a lot I can do for you. Let me make a few calls."

Brill and the others had arrived.

"Ready, gentlemen?"

Ballard said he'd pay the tab and went inside the café, a symphony of Belle Époque mirrors, marble counters, and gilded chandeliers.

Brill, meanwhile, was telling the others about the Gambrinus Café's history. How Hemingway had downed negronis at the bar. Pavarotti signed autographs while eating multiple pastries. Jean-Paul Sartre contemplated existence while watching a frozen *granita* melt into its enamel cup. Marcus noticed Ballard stumbling when he emerged from the café, nearly tripping over his own feet. And his expression changed, more intense than usual, his usual being happy-go-lucky. He quickly found his footing and met Marcus's eye with a wide grin.

They left the Gambrinus, following Brill as if he were a scout troop leader. It had been that way on several occasions during the conference when the professor knew of an excellent restaurant off the beaten track or a Caravaggio tucked away in a nearby church and he'd set off, trailed by several conference attendees. This was one last expedition, across the roundabout, passing the fountain in the shape of an artichoke, and onto the cobbled piazza that attracted scruffy kids, future Maradonas who chased soccer balls around tourists, the Argentine forward having starred for Napoli at the height of his career.

They walked by the Royal Palace wall and the eight statues of former kings of Naples, the oldest being the sword-wielding Roger II of Sicily, whose reign ended in 1154. Marcus stopped to take a bunch of photographs, as he'd done many times during the past few days. He broke into a light jog to catch up with the others.

The Royal Palace housed administrative offices, a museum, the National Library and, in a separate wing of the library, their destination: the Officina. At the main entrance, Brill said, "I'm afraid you're going to have to go through a bit of a security rigmarole." He breezed by the security kiosk while the others showed IDs and checked their bags into old wooden lockers. Then they climbed an elegantly sweeping staircase, arriving at the Biblioteca Nazionale Vittorio Emanuele III.

"This used to be the royal ballroom," Brill said softly in the ornate reading room. Gold-and-white bas-reliefs decorated the walls and vaulted ceiling. They continued through various chambers, passing large wooden globes, gilt cherubs with knowing, sensuous smiles, and archaic maps showing sea monsters and sinking ships. Tantalizing views of the Bay of Naples were glimpsed through windows.

The small group squeezed through corridors lined with heavy tomes and trudged up another flight of stairs. Finally, just beyond a sign that said *Papiri*, Brill led the way up a narrow flight of stone stairs that felt off-kilter. Maybe a secret passageway, Marcus thought, from the time of the Medici. It led to a windowless, concave chamber which gave way to yet another book-lined hallway. The labyrinthine journey ended in an austere room with a skylight and a large worktable outfitted with half a dozen microscopes. The Officina dei Papiri Ercolanesi.

There was a large, framed drawing of a Piaggio machine on one wall. It looked remarkably like the one Laszlo had built. The keys on the traction machine reminded Marcus of a cello and, by association, of a cellist from his college days; he'd met her at a party once, fell under her spell, and never saw her again aside from seeing her perform at concerts. Why did that snippet of his past remain vivid while so many others vanished? Was memory so arbitrary?

"Right," Brill said, clapping his hands once. "Let's have a look at the papyri." He briefly spoke in Italian with a middle-aged librarian with sharply etched lines in her narrow face. She clattered out of the room on high heels.

Brill turned to the little group and, directing his attention to the teenager, said, "Does anyone know where a papyrus scroll actually comes from?"

"From Egypt," said the retired British teacher. "Reeds from the Nile?"

"That's correct," Brill said. "The papyrus plant was found primarily in Egypt. It was harvested from marshes, its stalks cut into long, thin strips, which were placed vertically side by side, slightly overlapping each other, forming a sheet. Then another series of strips would be placed horizontally over that first sheet. The double-layered sheet was pounded with a mallet or passed through a press. The natural juice of the papyrus plant acted as an adhesive; the two layers were joined together. Several such sheets would then be attached width-wise to form a long horizontal row of papyrus paper that could be rolled into a scroll. The result was a roll that could be as long as twenty feet.

"And yet," Brill continued, "until a few hundred years ago, not one papyrus scroll, except for some scraps in the Egyptian desert, had survived history." He turned to a nearby glass vitrine, leaning on it as if it were a lectern. It contained several carbonized papyrus scrolls of various shapes and sizes.

Marcus eyed the blackened papyri in the display case: ungainly lumps, beaten-up chunks, broken cylinders — all variations of the woebegone specimen he'd inherited.

"These papyri," Brill said, "were found back in 1752, when diggers tunnelled down to what turned out to be an enormous Roman villa, a very, very luxurious villa, full of works of art, and a library. The only intact library discovered from the ancient world. It gave the Villa the name we use: the Villa dei Papiri. At first they thought these scrolls were just lumps of coal. They didn't realize they were books. But eventually a workman broke one open and saw the writing on the inside."

The American teenager asked, "How many of the scrolls here are still rolled up? I mean, how many have never been read?"

"There are about three hundred scrolls here, which are too damaged and bent out of shape to even attempt to unroll," Brill said. "The scrolls capable of being unrolled were unrolled a long time ago. And many, many were destroyed in the process, that's how fragile they are. It's been a long struggle to try to find the technology which would suffice to read them. There's been progress in recent years, to be sure. From microscopes to multi-spectral imaging. But it's slow going."

Ballard double-clicked on the issue. "Has anyone here tried virtual unrolling?"

"The silver bullet. Difficult, I'm afraid."

The librarian in high heels, perfume trailing in her wake, returned with a tray containing a sheet of papyrus. She carried the tray as if it was a platter of hors d'oeuvres.

"Ah," Brill said, "*grazie mille*, Lucrezia." He continued, "Perfect timing. Look at this fragment of one of the scrolls that was successfully unrolled and cut from the rest of the papyrus."

It resembled the segment of Gerald's scroll that Laszlo had glued to a board. Marcus had meant to get that text deciphered and translated before his trip, but his to-do list had expanded, and he never got round to it.

"See how close in colour a carbonized papyrus is to the ink that is written on it?" Brill continued. "And there lies the problem that has bedevilled these scrolls for centuries: insufficient contrast between the ink and the papyrus it's written on."

Ballard said, "The ink is charcoal mixed with water, and the papyrus is carbonized. So you're looking at black on black."

"Exactly."

"Has anyone tried X-ray phase-contrast tomography?" Ballard asked Brill. "It's used in medical imaging to get a picture of soft tissues that don't absorb X-rays very clearly, tissues like lungs and breasts. It works by detecting the contrast of how materials refract, as opposed to absorb, X-rays."

Marcus gazed up at the large glass skylight, and his thoughts drifted to his late uncle. Gerald would have loved this conversation. Marcus himself had a limited concentration span for anything scientific.

"We have tried regular medical X-rays," Brill said. "A team from the University of Kentucky X-rayed the scrolls a few years ago, but all we got was an incomprehensible alphabet soup of letters."

"I've been looking into this," Ballard said. "If your challenge is differentiating between papyrus and ink," he nodded to the display case, "according to a paper I read, the inked letters are in fact raised slightly. Not by much, about a tenth of a millimetre above the surface of the papyrus. But enough of a contrast, enough of a difference in the landscape of the scroll, that it might show up when beaming X-rays from a particle accelerator facility. I think this might work."

"Well," Brill said. "That's above my pay grade. I leave that to you."

"I'll see what I can do," Ballard said, flashing a smile to Brill and then to Marcus.

Confiding in Ballard about Gerald's scroll was the right move, Marcus thought. Despite all his kidding around, the Google engineer clearly knew his stuff. The scroll would be in good hands with him.

The hedge fund manager said, "Playing the devil's advocate here for my son, who asked me why we care so much. I mean, why go to all this trouble if these things are so damn difficult to unroll?"

"Well, that's not an unreasonable question," Brill replied, turning to the teenager. "For starters, it's important to remember in this context just how many ancient books have been lost. History, science, poetry — everything. Valuable lessons from the past are missing. Bear in mind that a great playwright like Sophocles, for example, wrote some one hundred plays, and only seven have survived. What if one of these scrolls contains another play by Sophocles? It's the same for nearly all the great writers and thinkers of antiquity. There's a tremendous amount of material to recover."

Marcus mused about Gerald's scroll. The Herculaneum scrolls that had been unrolled were written mostly in Greek, mostly Epicurean philosophy, with a smattering of very damaged fragments in Latin. Gerald's scroll was in Latin. There were so many ancient authors who could spring to life from that chunk of charcoal: Cicero, Livy, and Octavian were all on Marcus's wish list.

"Now, let's have a closer look," Brill said, "through a microscope."

He invited Marcus, who was standing nearest, to take a seat at the reading room table. Brill removed a segment of unrolled papyrus from the tray. There were holes, tears, and buckles on the darkened papyrus. Brill slid the segment underneath a high-powered Zeiss microscope and fiddled with its controls. He showed Marcus how to adjust the focus.

"Whatever you do, don't sneeze on the papyrus. I don't care about germs, but about the text getting blown away."

Marcus swept his hair away from his face and leaned his head onto the microscope eyepiece. He didn't see anything. He twisted the focus knob back and forth: still, nothing but blackness. Aware that everyone was expecting a reaction, he kept adjusting the focus. Whenever some sort of image briefly appeared, it was like looking out the window of an airplane at a mountain range with jagged ridges, pockmarked with craters and splotched with lakes. He sometimes worried in-flight about planes crashing, but being able to see anything terrestrial from the plane, whether rooftops or mountain ranges, reassured him and eased the worry. *Terra firma.*

He was jolted back to the moment by letters, Greek letters, beautiful letters, that suddenly swam into focus: elegant black forms dancing in the dusk.

"I see letters! Incredible. It took a while, but now I can see them."

The others took turns peering into the papyrus. Ballard was the last person up, and Marcus snapped a photo of him with one of

Ballard's eyes lodged on the viewfinder, the other wide open for the photo, like a Cyclops.

Marcus had snapped many pics of Ballard during the conference. They'd emailed each other their best shots. Ballard in the Umberto shopping gallery, grinning widely and holding aloft a *sfogliatella* pastry stuffed with ricotta and candied citrus. Ballard at a twelve-course pizza-tasting meal, planting a kiss on the forehead of an elderly waitress. Flashing a peace sign on the moonscape that was Mount Vesuvius. Kneeling beside an astonishing marbled sculpture of a veiled Jesus. On the waterfront, brandishing a gelato with pine nuts and sesame. But the photo of Ballard's head tilted on a high-powered microscope, about to view a sheet of papyrus, was the last image Marcus would ever take of him.

4

CENTRO STORICO

"**Y**ou saw him the day he was murdered?"

"Yes. We met for a coffee that morning. At the Caffè Mexico."

"Caffè Mexico. In Piazza Dante?"

"Yes."

"What time?"

"Around nine o'clock."

Detective Giuseppe Cimma wore a two-day growth of beard, a crisp blue shirt, and a neutral expression that verged on boredom. Marcus was being questioned in a drab interrogation room on the third floor of police headquarters on Via Toledo. Third floor, he thought, the same level as Ballard's hotel room, where he had been found dead two days earlier.

"What did you talk about?"

"Nothing special. But he told me he was having lunch with a scientist."

"A scientist?"

"Yes. But I don't know who. He didn't go into details."

Marcus had given his scroll to Ballard, who'd promised to get it back to him in about one week's time. It would not be physically unrolled, he said, but virtually unrolled. Digitally deciphered. Before that could happen, he was found dead. Murdered, the police said, though they were short on specifics.

Marcus could count his real friendships on one hand, and although he had known Ballard for all of one week, he'd gotten close to the man, felt in synch with him, and had every reason to think they would stay in touch. Their brief friendship had somehow chipped away at something that had felt like a layer of glass encasing him since Gerald's death. This new death — a murder, no less — was sickening.

And now Gerald's scroll was gone. Marcus had checked with the Officina. His vague questions raised eyebrows but turned up nothing that had belonged to Trevor Ballard. So it was well and truly gone. Unless the police had it.

Why had he given the scroll to Ballard? Even *bringing* the thing to Italy now seemed like a bone-headed move! He could have just brought photos of the papyrus along with a photocopy of the segment that Laszlo had unrolled. He'd actually lent Ballard the photocopy as well, and it too was gone. Or in police hands.

His personal loss paled in comparison with the horror of Ballard's death. Still, he had to pursue it.

"I was wondering," Marcus said. "I had lent Mr. Ballard a papyrus scroll. Did the police find it among his possessions?"

"A papyrus?" the detective asked. "Why did you give it to him?"

"I brought it with me to Italy. I was hoping to get some help unrolling it. He had some good ideas about how to do that."

"No," Officer Cimma said, checking his cell phone. "There was nothing like that in his hotel room."

Marcus folded his arms so that his right hand rested on his left bicep and the fingers of his other hand tucked beneath his right bicep.

It was a comfortable position. But he wondered whether it looked defensive, as if he had something to hide, so he untangled his arms. His legs were jiggling under the table. He put the brakes on that too.

"Or a photocopy showing Latin writing? I also lent him that."

The detective ignored that question, seeming satisfied with the interview or just uninterested. "*Grazie*," he said, "we will call you if we have more questions." He glanced down at the desk holding a list of names from the Friends of Herculaneum conference. Most had left Italy by now, but he still had time to follow up with a few more potential witnesses.

On his way out, Marcus saw Olivier Auger and two others from the conference, a British classics prof and a German archaeologist, waiting their turns to be questioned.

"How was it?" Auger asked.

"Quick and painless."

"Let's hope that's how Ballard died," said the German.

Outside, a mild sea breeze was blowing on Via Toledo as a throng of people made its way along the pedestrianized street. A lone gull was picking at something in the broken seam of a cobblestone. Ballard was dead. At first it had seemed so unreal to Marcus, it didn't quite register. Now that it felt real, a knot of anxiety had formed in his gut. He looked at some peeling plaster on the nondescript police building and turned his gaze upwards. *Quick and painless.* Why had he even said that? There was nothing painless about what had happened, what was happening. He wasn't in his right mind.

He checked his phone messages. Nothing. He slowly walked up Toledo to the Piazza Dante and stopped outside the café called Mexico. Its facade was garish, as if wrapped in tin foil. Marcus hesitated, then passed under an orange awning and into a tiny joint crammed with coffee-making products for sale. He paid the cashier and handed the receipt to a barista wearing a white coat with flashy epaulets and the white cap of a short order cook. The ceiling lights projected an oddly psychedelic orange glow. Behind the bar, a hulking espresso machine, its five handles protruding, was also bright orange. All told, the decor was a nonsensical imagining of Mexico, but the coffee was stellar.

At the counter, he nursed an espresso and chased it with a small glass of fizzy water. He had last seen Ballard at this very spot, sipping espressos, as they'd done many times before on this trip. After they'd drained their coffees, Ballard's phone rang and, taking the call, he said to Marcus, "Talk soon" as they parted company. Just two days ago he was alive, brimming with vitality, leaning on this same counter. How could he be gone? Marcus felt a double loss — Ballard and the scroll — and felt ashamed for fretting about the scroll, a mere *thing*. Why would anyone want to kill Ballard? And what exactly happened to the poor soul?

Still, he had to wonder why he'd so quickly entrusted the papyrus to Ballard. He cursed his stupidity in not being more vigilant. It was such careless treatment of something he actually cared about. And there weren't many such things in his life. He had no right to be raging at the fates. He was alive. He was free from financial worries. But free to do what?

Marcus exited the café and crossed to Piazza Dante, where a statue of the immortal poet struck him as just one more Neapolitan saintly figure with an outstretched arm. Begging, beseeching, or bestowing: he couldn't say. The base of the statue was riddled with graffiti; there were pigeons and trash and churches and everywhere the Bourbon dynasty's colour scheme of peach and grey. There was a medieval spookiness to the city when the sun wasn't shining, a Dark Ages atmosphere of saints and gargoyles, crumbling plaster and decrepit shrines, and Marcus felt a rancid sickness in his core.

He dragged himself across the piazza and through the clocktower archway to a passage lined with booksellers. Marcus skirted the Piazza Bellini with its café parasols and clouds of hashish, past the university music faculty where the desolate murmurs of a cello echoed his state of mind. He pressed on through Via dei Tribunali, ignoring the pastries and pizza, weaving through the crowd and mindful of darting motorbikes.

His new five-star hotel was in a dignified palazzo on a quiet side street. Since the conference in Herculaneum had ended, he'd started spending more of Gerald's money. Ballard also had money to spend, so they'd relocated to the same high-end hotel in Naples. All Marcus wanted to do now was collapse on the plush bed, with its harem's worth of pillows and a velvety headboard.

He slid the keycard into the slot, opened the door, and was jolted by a chaotic scene. His suitcase, which he hadn't unpacked, was flung open, its contents strewn across the wood floor. Someone had been in a hurry to go through his things. There was nothing to find there, nothing left of value, but the shock of this invasion rattled nerves already on edge. He checked the bathroom, the closet, even under the bed. Whoever had been in his room was obviously gone. Heartbeat gunning every red light in his body, he was on the verge of a panic attack. He locked the door and fastened the chain. He sank into the bed and thought of that bucket-list slogan from the nineteenth century: *See Naples and Die.*

He'd seen Naples. He was ready to leave.

5

CHIAIA

Carmela Zuccarello downshifted her Vespa, leaned into a roundabout, and stopped at a red light at the Piazza del Plebiscito. Two other scooters flanked the homicide squad chief, revving their engines and awaiting the traffic signal as if it were a starter's pistol. The light turned green, and the buzzing motorbikes flew off: not for nothing does *vespa* mean wasp.

A case involving a busload of foreigners — two busloads, actually — not to mention Google, was sensitive, meaning Zuccarello preferred to keep lower-level police out of the picture. She'd left the basic interviews to one of her subordinates, a homicide cop she'd been sleeping with until a few weeks ago. But Zuccarello didn't trust Giuseppe for higher-level detective work, and her degree in criminology from the University of Miami equipped her with very serviceable English. So, for a key interview with an expat American, she took matters into her own hands, got out of her dreary office, and battled through chaotic traffic on her scooter.

She should never have started things with Giuseppe, who was nowhere near as bright, or as old, as his boss and, truth be told, was fundamentally vapid. She had hoped for an efficient arrangement; much too quickly, he had become besotted. Now she couldn't bear his stream of syrupy text messages.

She really should get a handle on her libido. Control the damn thing as well as she controlled the motorbike. But the demands of the job and limited free time didn't exactly add up to a judicious dispensation of her own sexual favours. *Judicious?* The word must contain the Latin root for "well judged." One day, perhaps, she'd get a judgeship or a prosecutor posting. But for now, she'd have to content herself with catching criminals. And exercising better judgment with lovers.

Zuccarello considered the sparse details of the homicide. Mr. Trevor Ballard, a forty-four-year-old computer engineer for Google. Attending the "Friends of Herculaneum" conference in Ercolano, populated by painfully serious, mostly British professors trooping around with their safari hats and maps. No witnesses, yet a hotel surveillance camera showed a man in a wide-brimmed hat and dark sunglasses leaving the Hotel Partenope at the assumed time of the killing. Ballard's laptop and phone were missing. And two pairs of nitrile gloves were found in his room's trash basket.

There wasn't much to go on. But among Mr. Ballard's belongings retrieved from the hotel was a scrap of paper with a phone number for an American man named Sweeney. The phone number had led the murder squad chief and her scooter to a leafy section of the upscale Chiaia neighbourhood. She parked outside an elegantly renovated palazzo. She would love to live in an area like this, civilized, away from the godforsaken suburbs with their rock-bottom prices and sky-high crime, real crime, Camorra-level crime. One day, if she ever got appointed judge. If a fucked-up system could tilt just a little in her favour. God knew she'd paid her dues. Checked all the career boxes, including a master's degree in law on top of everything else. Now all she could do was wait. And do her job.

The name of Thomas J. Sweeney was engraved on a polished bronze plaque near the imposing double door. There was no doorbell, so Zuccarello banged twice on a brass knocker shaped like a coiled snake.

An assistant, or valet, or whatever, answered the door, and she was struck by the man's handsome, angular face, close-cropped hair, and muscular build. That's what she needed: a lover far removed from her workplace. Presumably, he had instructions to expect her because without asking for her name, he said, "Mr. Sweeney will see you in the *tablinum*."

Tablinum?

The man silently ushered her through a corridor lined with portrait masks. Nice touch. She knew her Italian history: the masks were meant to be the homeowner's forebears going back a few generations, echoing a standard element of ancient Roman decor. She was beginning to understand the *tablinum* reference.

The dark corridor opened onto an atrium so dazzling she needed to shield her eyes: a rectangular pool with statues gracing each corner, a murmuring fountain shaped like a peacock, and a mosaic floor patterned with black-and-white geometric designs, all illuminated by a vast skylight.

She followed the muscular man along a marble floor, past a bronze statue of a frolicking piglet, to another room. They entered a sort of reception hall with walls veneered with sheets of marble or plaster painted in imitation of marble; either way, it was impressive.

"Please, make yourself comfortable," Thomas Sweeney said, walking slowly with a cane from the opposite end of the room. He appeared to be in his late seventies, with a trim white beard, wire-rimmed glasses, and what little remained of his hair tightly combed back. He was wearing a loosely fitting ivory shirt with a Mao collar, which, given the surroundings, made Zuccarello think of a toga.

"Carmela Zuccarello, Naples police, criminal investigation division," she said, extending her hand.

He responded by fluttering his fingers at a hard-backed chair. Zuccarello took the seat he had indicated, and with some effort, Sweeney eased his stiff frame onto the couch facing her. He loosened his grip on his walking stick, which was topped with a lion's head.

The notes prepared by the office librarian explained that thirty-odd years ago, Sweeney had founded a blandly named organization that operated as a "university without walls" where researchers carried out interdisciplinary research. Among the inventions that resulted were the PalmPilot, various artificial intelligence breakthroughs, and the simulation of neural networks for image recognition software. The group had also incubated PurpleProse, an app which made ebooks easy to read on tablets. A few Silicon Valley companies, Google included, licensed its products.

"You have a beautiful home, Mr. Sweeney."

"I put a lot of work into it. A faithful replica of an ancient Roman *domus*. However, I'm not entirely stuck in the past. Upstairs there are modern rooms. But enough about me and my anachronistic architecture. What brings you here? Are the mean streets of Naples no longer sufficiently criminal?"

"I'm investigating the death here of an American tourist named Trevor Ballard."

"Oh yes, Mr. Ballard. A terrible tragedy. The Friends of Herculaneum sent out an email. But what, may I ask again, brings you here?"

"Your name and phone number were found on a piece of paper in Mr. Ballard's hotel room. Why would he have your number?"

"A lot of people in the tech world know my name," said Sweeney. He removed his eyeglasses and carefully wiped the lenses with a tissue. "Ballard sought me out, and we met. We talked shop, as it were. I have an interest in technology that could be of use in some of the projects he was working on. The press reports say he was murdered. I find that hard to believe. What really happened?"

"The circumstances are under investigation."

"Terrible."

"What sort of technology were you discussing with Mr. Ballard?"

"I can't get into details. But it's no secret that Ballard wanted to harness Google's technology to unroll scrolls from the Villa at Herculaneum."

"You mean the old papyri from the Officina?"

"Yes. But the Officina is a veritable Fort Knox, if you know what I mean. No scrolls come in or out of there. And they would be unlikely to let outsiders set up shop in situ with the sort of technology that Ballard wanted to use."

On a wooden stand beside his couch was a small bronze bell in the form of a drunken satyr. Sweeney jingled the bell. "Nonius," he said when his employee appeared. "Wine for two."

"Thank you," Zuccarello said, "a glass of water will be fine."

"The wine is highly diluted."

"I don't drink while I'm working, thank you. When was the last time you saw Mr. Ballard?"

"A week ago. At one of the Herculaneum conference dinners. The Saturday night dinner. You know the restaurant Tubba Catubba in Ercolano? The whole crew was there. I put in an appearance and had one glass of prosecco. But I was feeling under the weather and did not stay for the actual dinner."

"Did you discuss anything in particular?"

"Nothing much. I asked him how he was finding the conference. He was enthusiastic. Everyone there seemed to want to engage him in conversation."

"Was anyone there hostile to him?"

"Not that I could see. It was quite the opposite, if you ask me."

"And before then? When did you first meet Mr. Ballard?"

"Oh, I don't recall exactly. Advanced age does a number on short-term memory, I'm afraid. But all my meetings are recorded in my calendar. I can have Nonius email you the information."

"Please do. Your name is also on the conference list for the Friends of Herculaneum. You are a 'marble-level' member. Did anything interesting happen at the conference this year?"

"I was not at the conference aside from that one dinner. I can't handle the heat anymore while traipsing around the ruins or listening to interminable lectures. However, I am supportive of the Friends of Herculaneum. They are brethren. Fellow believers."

"Believers?"

"I spent many years chasing the tail of technology, always pushing for more and more innovations, forever focused on the future. Then I moved here and recalibrated my life according to the doctrines of Epicurus. Avoiding pain and anxiety. Finding pleasure in tranquility, friendship, and wisdom. So I gravitate, naturally, to the Friends of Herculaneum."

Sweeney lifted the satyr bell and gave it another ring.

"There is more. I support the Friends, yes, with my 'marble-level' funds, because I consider Herculaneum a worthy cause. Where else might we find so many ancient works, masterpieces quite possibly, otherwise lost to history? Nowhere. At least not to this degree. It's a scandal that archaeologists are not digging at this very moment when almost all of the Villa dei Papiri is languishing underground."

The employee named Nonius caught her eye again, appearing with a tray holding two earthenware cups, a glass decanter of wine, and a jug of water.

"Add a bit of water to my glass," Sweeney instructed. "Just water for the officer."

Zuccarello noticed the assistant's hand grazing Sweeney's shoulder and found herself wondering about their relationship. Then Nonius left the room. Stop, she told herself. Focus on the matter at hand.

Sweeney said, "Did you know that when the Villa dei Papiri was found it was the largest private Roman villa ever discovered? If it were a real estate listing today, it would be advertised as a multi-storey villa measuring more than two hundred thousand square feet. Featuring a colonnaded garden, a pool, a grand peristyle with fountains, a fishpond, a belvedere overlooking the Bay of Naples, and a terraced access to the beach below."

Satisfied with this rich nugget of information, he took a sip of wine and unfastened the top button of his Mao collar.

Was he deliberately changing the subject, leading her down a rabbit hole? Or was his mind just addled with age? She asked him: "Did Mr. Ballard also want to excavate the Villa for more *papiri*?"

Sweeney shifted his gaze, looking dreamily into his glass of diluted wine. "He was new to this game. And his interest was in any case purely technological."

"But your interests are also technological, no?"

"I'm afraid that gets into my business arrangements, which are confidential. Non-disclosure agreements and so on."

Nonius entered the room, and her line of questioning was derailed. Ever since she cut things off with Giuseppe, her mind had been wandering in such directions.

"It's actually time for my afternoon nap," Sweeney said. "Being seventy-nine has its perks. But do keep in touch."

That was fine with Zuccarello, given the many peripheral tangents the conversation with Sweeney seemed to entail. She got to her feet and leaned over to hand him her professional card.

"Thank you, Mr. Sweeney. Please email me info about those meetings with Mr. Ballard. I may be in touch again."

"Any time at all, Miss Zuccarello. You know where to find me."

Nonius led the officer back out through the dazzling atrium. She passed a table, its legs crafted to look like those of a horse, and what seemed to be chimes hanging from each end, except the chime bells were in fact hanging from what appeared to be bronze phalluses with wings. More sex. But not of her own conjuring. As her gaze lingered on the table, she noticed a package sitting on it addressed in bold block letters to PurplePapyrus.

6

TORONTO

Marcus barely registered a presence on social media, guarding his privacy against evil algorithms and miscellaneous voyeurism. He never shared, liked, or posted anything. He didn't lead the sort of life which lent itself to online chronicling — no milestones involving kids, no trumpeting his affection for music, cuisine, pets, or politics. He was just there, living a low-profile existence, gathering digital dust. What was the Epicurean credo? *Live unnoticed.* Well, he'd mastered that art.

Back home in Toronto, he was at a barber shop waiting his turn when he checked his Facebook account for the first time in ages. There was a message from a journalist named Kristi Grainger. Another scam artist, no doubt. He nearly deleted the message straight off. But a closer look — her profile pic was not unattractive — suggested the message was legitimate. She was looking for information about the death of a Google engineer in Italy, had apparently checked the membership list of the Friends of Herculaneum and spotted the name of someone local. So much for living unnoticed.

He had time to peruse her profile as his barber had fallen behind schedule. Appointments were almost always delayed at Hair of the Dog, which oddly featured a Norton 850 Commando motorcycle as decor. The barbers themselves cultivated a rugged look, four heavily tattooed men who would have been lumberjacks or Visigoth warriors in another era. They appeared to be there not so much for their customers as to entertain one another. The quartet of coiffeurs were currently bellowing back and forth on the subject of hangovers.

Marcus scanned Kristi Grainger's online profile, so much more fleshed-out than his own. She'd been a reporter at the *Toronto Star* for decades and was apparently now on some sort of journalism fellowship. Professional awards, social justice causes, hot yoga, spin classes, and a college-age kid. The sort of living-life-to-the-max that Marcus couldn't claim, online or off.

His barber was taking his sweet time. Among the man's tattoos was that old-fashioned symbol, a barber's pole, inked impressively on the side of his neck. Marcus's long hair would have covered such a tattoo. The only part of his body that seemed to be defying the gravity of age was his hair. But it got messy in areas he couldn't himself handle without nicking an ear or the back of his neck or skewing a sideburn. A trim was regularly needed.

Kristi Grainger had replied to his reply and was trying to set up a meeting. Why not? He had nothing to hide. He was still very much puzzled and troubled by Trevor Ballard's death. And pissed about losing Gerald's scroll. His head kept spinning about that. There seemed no conceivable way to get it back. It was no more likely than Ballard coming back to life.

He agreed to meet at a café. Message sent, he looked up from his phone. The shop was festooned with posters of motorcycles and punk rock bands. His barber was fussing over a carrot-top client while launching one-liners laced with F-bombs. Maybe all the drink-till-I-puke machismo was designed to counterbalance so much effeminate preening.

Marcus eyed the bottles of beard ointment, after-shave cologne, straight razors, and shaving brushes. He could use one of those old-timey shaves, porcelain chair swivelled back, piping hot cream foaming his face. Yet he wouldn't trust his distracted barber to wield a straight razor. The image triggered anxiety related to his stolen scroll, Trevor Ballard's death, his own hotel room in Naples being ransacked. A shudder ran through him before he realized his name was finally being called.

His barber, Andy, gave a brisk sweep of the porcelain chair and spun it around for Marcus to sit down. After fastening the white smock around his client's neck, Andy went to the cash register. Marcus repositioned his stocky frame so that he was sitting straighter. Looking at his reflection in the mirror, he glimpsed something Gerald-like but wasn't sure exactly what it was. It had been more than four months since his uncle had died. Marcus's hazel eyes, set far apart, were registering fatigue more than anything else. Brown hair threaded with silver grazed his shoulders. It seemed like only yesterday that he was ten, fifteen, twenty years younger, his hair without a single strand of grey. In the blink of two decades, he'd be seventy-one, arthritic, stooped, his hair, if he still had any, gone entirely silver. A blink or two after that and — that unforgiving marble floor in Gerald's bathroom came to mind — game over.

HE MET KRISTI GRAINGER THE NEXT DAY at the Tampered Press on Dundas Street West. The café was filled with laptop-pecking youth drinking out of mason jars at a large, rough-hewn table that might have been a salvaged barn door. Kristi had jet-black hair laced with burgundy streaks, which made her look a fair bit younger and funkier than Marcus felt himself to be. She wore stretchy grey pants with a bit of a flare above turquoise sneakers. A baby-blue yoga mat jutted out of her knapsack.

Kristi said, "How about we get our coffees to go? We can talk in the park."

They crossed the street to a park bench beside a bust of Simón Bolívar. The South American liberator seemed to be glaring at the café from a distance.

"Weird statue to be here," Marcus said. "And a strange scowl on his face. As if he disapproves of our gringo coffees."

The joke fell flat; Kristi managed a polite chuckle.

"So, as I mentioned, I'm writing a story about Trevor Ballard."

"Well, I barely knew him, though we got along great. We met in Italy, at the conference, about three weeks ago."

"The fact that he was murdered has to be tough nonetheless," she said. "I'm sorry. But can I ask you a few background questions?"

"Sure. And his death *was* shocking. Not that I know any details. All that the Italian media and the police said was that he was murdered. But can I ask what you're going to do with the story? Who are you writing it for?"

Kristi was just getting used to answering this question differently than had been the case the previous two decades. She'd been happy at the *Star* until her career was flatlined by the internet because readers grabbed their news online for free and advertisers abandoned print. The result was newsroom jobs cut to the bone. She was given less time to write and often saddled with assignments that were dull as boiled cabbage. Even worse, reporters were now expected to produce visual clips to go with their stories and to constantly post tweets the length of fortune cookie prophecies. So far as she could see, the newspaper was kowtowing to Facebook, Amazon, and Google, selling its soul for so many clicks. In a desperate bid for eyeballs, the old media now courted algorithms in search of likes and shares.

She had finally left the *Star* after a cancer scare. It turned out to be a false positive but was sufficiently unnerving that she eventually accepted the buyout package offered to all editorial staff. The time was right. Her son had finished university in Vancouver and was working for a startup. There would be more time for yoga and meditation. And she had snagged a prestigious fellowship which paid handsomely and entailed writing a single in-depth feature. She figured she found that feature story when an online discussion group about looted antiquities tipped her off about Ballard. The mysterious death of a Google engineer in Italy, ancient papyrus scrolls, leading-edge technology: these were potentially the right ingredients for the sort of multi-layered investigative story she was looking for.

"I'm on a Michener fellowship this year," she told Marcus, "and am writing one long investigative story. I've left the *Star*, but that's where my article will be published. I once wrote a series about looted antiquities that the Royal Ontario Museum had to return, and I'm still interested in the subject."

Marcus remembered reading those articles, attuned to anything about antiquities because of Gerald's line of work.

"So," she said, opening a small spiral notepad, "did you notice any friction between Ballard and anyone else at the conference?"

"No. It was a friendly group. Ballard's presence seemed to be very welcome. In fact, the academics flocked around him at every opportunity. They kept whispering things about him, like a rumour that he had invented Gmail."

"He got a lot of attention?"

"In a low-key way. It seemed to be a general feeling that he — that's to say, Google — represented a huge amount of resources which might be injected into Herculaneum. The site needs it. The scrolls need it. Everyone seemed to be on the same page about that."

Skateboarders zipped by, tumbling, jumping, falling, their ambition outpacing their skills.

"Did Ballard have any run-ins with anyone at the event?"

"None that I know of."

An image of his tattooed barber suddenly popped into Marcus's mind, and then he remembered the tattooed archaeologist from the conference. "Hold on — there was a seriously drunk archaeologist sounding off about Google's presence in Herculaneum. We were at the opening event, a meet and greet. The guy was fulminating against Google. Google and Ballard."

"Do you remember his name?"

"No. He was Greek, I think. And part American. Yeah, I remember he made a point of saying that. His English was perfect. And he had a ton of tattoos from his neck to his knuckles."

"What sort of tattoos?"

"Archaeological symbols. Shovels and trowels, that sort of thing, as well as Greek letters."

He recounted what he remembered of the man's drunken tirade. As she wrote in her notepad, Marcus noticed she was wearing a necklace of tiny glass beads and shells.

"Interesting," she said. "And if I understand correctly, there's an ongoing dispute between the papyrologists and the archaeologists."

"What do you mean by that?"

"You know, the archaeologists want to preserve the existing site of Herculaneum. Versus the papyrologists, who want to put money into digging to look for more scrolls."

"That simplifies things. It's complicated. Besides, Ballard wanted to use new technologies to decipher those scrolls that had already been dug up. He didn't have much to say about further digging."

"Yes, but," she was writing in her small notepad, her fingernails painted the colour of a peach, "let's assume his tech idea to decipher the scrolls actually worked. Wouldn't that be an incentive to excavate more?"

"That's true. But presumably any new excavation would be a long way off."

Kristi said, "It sounds to me like there's a rift between these factions. The pro-diggers against those who want to preserve the site as is."

"I never thought of it quite so neatly," Marcus said. As he spoke, an image of Gerald's blackened scroll popped into his head. "There's one other thing," he said. "I had a papyrus scroll with me in Italy. I lent it to Ballard. He was going to help me decipher the scroll. When he died, it disappeared, and I never got it back."

Kristi looked up from her writing. "You had a scroll? From Herculaneum?"

"Yes. At least, I assume it was from there. I never had it professionally authenticated. But that's what it has to be. Or had to have been."

"Hmmm," she said, finally looking up from her notepad. "That *is* interesting. I'm sorry you lost it. What else can you tell me about this?"

Marcus recounted the whole story: Gerald's bequest, Laszlo and the Piaggio machine, his own hope to get the scroll unrolled in Naples, and the ill-fated loan of the object to Trevor Ballard.

"It breaks my heart," he said. "I mean, I don't know what exactly happened to Trevor, to Ballard, but it's awful, devastating. And separately, less tragically, of course, the fact that I lost the scroll, which my uncle seemed to treasure, and left to me very deliberately, well, losing the thing . . ."

He didn't finish the sentence, pausing to look at Kristi Grainger. Her eyes widened, and she sounded an "umhmm" while scribbling more words. Every note of his sorry saga seemed to be recorded in her notepad. Plus she was as attractive as her Facebook profile pics suggested.

"I'm really sorry for your loss," she said. "All these losses."

Was he overstating his losses? Having known Trevor Ballard for all of one week, could Marcus legitimately call him a friend? It seemed like he could. His friends were all friends in a specific context. Childhood friends, teacher friends, tennis friends, neighbourhood friends, ex-girlfriend friends. So what was Ballard? A Herculaneum friend. A murdered friend.

A pigeon approached their bench, and Marcus shooed it away.

"Regarding the murder," she said. "I've called the municipal police in Naples, the *polizia*, and have gotten nowhere."

"Did you check with the Officina, you know, the papyrus lab? He was regularly in touch with the people there."

"I checked. Ballard was not registered as working in the Officina that day." She put her iPhone, pen, and notepad away into a small bag with shoulder straps.

"One other thing," Kristi said. "Did Ballard have any, ah, intimate relationships while in Naples?"

"Not that I know of. I doubt it."

"Why is that?"

"He didn't give off that vibe."

Marcus thought, *Am I giving off that vibe?* He ruffled his hair.

"After dinner," Kristi said, "he's back at the hotel. Who knows what pleasures he decided to indulge in? Let's not forget we're talking about an Epicurean conference."

"Not that kind of Epicureanism."

"I thought there was only one kind."

"You mean five-star meals and fine wine? The pursuit of pleasure? Not quite," Marcus said. "That's the modern version. The conference was about the classical philosophy, which prized tranquility. Philosophy. And scholarship."

7

OFFICINA

David Brill adjusted the microscope to account for the sunshine streaming in from the skylight of the Officina. Always so sharp, this sun! If only his own powers of illumination could be so flawless.

Instead, it was one Greek letter after another, one lacuna after another, blank spaces slowly filling in with letters, or hypothetical characters, placeholder words, theories — whatever he could muster, one summer after another, always coming back to this storied city. Always returning to this monumental jigsaw puzzle. Twenty-six summers devoted to a single text.

His work was weather-dependent. Sunlight was the most indispensable piece of his equipment. Even an overcast day would obscure the image. And the winter sun was not strong enough, meaning his work was limited to Neapolitan summers. When faced with an especially murky letter, Brill would remove his glasses and place a black eye patch over one eye, the better to focus with the other. Even his eyeglasses had side flaps to prevent light from intruding on his field of vision. Out on the raucous streets of Naples, these glasses combined with his safari hat gave him the look of an explorer. Which is how he viewed himself. An explorer of ancient texts, hacking his way through an alphabetic jungle.

Brill heard a rustling of paper and looked across the room to see Christoph turning the pages of a fat reference book. The German scholar was only just beginning his post-doc fellowship. How many summers would he last? He was a square peg in the round hole that was Italy. Stiff and awkward, with limited Italian. *Twenty-six years ago*, thought Brill, *I was more or less the same. But even then, my Italian was far better.*

Lorenzo, the Italian Ph.D. student squinting into a microscope nearby, was so much sleeker, more stylish, more comfortable in his own skin. It was a wonder that a good-looking Italian with an energetic social life would opt for the cloistered career of a papyrologist.

In the past, the Italians did not make the best papyrologists, though there had always been exceptions. The dynamo who founded the Officina, Marcello Gigante, had encouraged the use of scientific techniques to decipher the papyri. He also did more than anyone else to open study of the scrolls to international scholarship. Initially it was the Germans who'd made the most progress. But that was changing, happily. The field could use more of the local and historical knowledge the Italians were providing, as well as more technology, which was slowly being supplied by the Americans.

Brill's gaze drifted to a framed poster on the wall, which declared the motto of the International Committee of Papyrology: *amicitia papyrologorum*, "the friendship of papyrologists." No one scholar is more important than the field at large. Every papyrologist stands on the shoulders of his forebears.

He looked one last time at the reconstructed Greek sentence he'd been spending all week on:

αὔριον — εἰςλιτήν σε καλιάδα, φίλτατε Πείσων —
ἐξένάτηςἔλκει μουσοφιλὴς ἕταρος,
εἰκάδα δειπνίζων ἐνιαύσιον· εἰ δ᾽ — ὄψει παναληθέας,
ἀλλ᾽ ἐπακούσῃ —
πουλὺ μελιχρότερα —
εἰκάδα πιοτέρην.

His text was by Philodemus: Book Two of *On Friendship*. The passage appeared to be celebrating friendship as the greatest blessing of all in life. Only about half the original text had survived, and what survived was in fragments. A dozen different scrolls contained the text, along with about two hundred disparate pieces of papyrus, and the transcriptions known as *disegni* made a century ago by copyists before the fragile originals crumbled.

It was a vast puzzle. Brill compared photographs of the text with colour slides from a CD-ROM enhanced by Adobe Photoshop. He examined sheets of papyrus from various angles via a binocular microscope and augmented those with multi-spectral images of the text. He had to think in three dimensions, like an archaeologist with a shattered amphora, matching the jumbled fragments by shape, colour, and design. All told it was, as he was fond of saying to anyone who asked, "a nightmarish riddle." This would be the crowning work of his career. Maybe afterwards he'd go back to his first love, Socrates, and finish his days at his college office in Oxford. But he would dearly miss the gorgeous light, the sweet arias emanating from the San Carlo opera house next door, and much else of *la bella Napoli*.

He packed up his things like a dutiful schoolboy. Half a dozen blue pencils, red pen, eraser, ruler, magnifying glass. Eye drops, notebook, and a part of his copy of the scroll for *On Friendship*. It was an absurdly long photocopy of the scroll in dozens of sections, taped together, with enhanced imaging. The full copy measured 49.2 feet in total, representing 76.3 layers of the scroll, and was adorned with copious corrections, musings, and marginalia.

There was only one efficient way to work with such an unwieldy mass of paper: he rolled a portion of it, several feet representing his latest work, into a scroll, coming full circle technologically with the ancients. He placed the rolled-up photocopy along with his other work items in his blue knapsack and nodded goodbyes to Christoph and Lorenzo, glued to their respective microscopes.

Once outside the Royal Palace, Brill crossed the roundabout with the artichoke fountain, made his way by the Caffè Gambrinus, and strode briskly up Via Toledo. Despite his annual visits to Naples, he continued to marvel at the panache of the locals. A Neapolitan was easily identified, even in the crowded thoroughfare that Toledo was on a Friday afternoon.

The ancient Greeks, who founded Naples and called it "Parthenope," prized the quality of *Aglaia* in art — a sparkly brightness, the glitter of divinity. The local women often had something golden or silvery shimmering on their shoes. Or they wore stiletto heels despite the treacherous cobblestones. The men, Brill noted, wore their collars jauntily turned up on their polo shirts. Subtle embellishments, setting the Neapolitans apart from obvious tourists. Men also lounged on parked scooters, sidesaddle on their plush seats, chatting no less comfortably than on their sofas at home. Other scooters whizzed by, somehow avoiding pedestrians, though safety did not appear to be a priority. They transported one or two, sometimes three family members, the youngest squeezed up against the handlebars and occasionally doing some of the steering.

Brill made his way up Toledo, his knapsack slung over one shoulder. He passed the big beige-and-grey Banco di Napoli headquarters as the smooth flagstones on the street gave way to small, roughly pitted cobblestones. He turned left up a side street that led into the claustrophobic working-class neighbourhood known as the Quartieri

Spagnoli, where the tottering buildings, tenements and dilapidated palazzi, closed in on the narrow street like overstocked shelves of library stacks. Balconies held washing that might effortlessly be stolen were it not so threadbare. Wall shrines that commemorated departed loved ones were carved into brick facades and filled with electric candles, photos, and plaster Madonnas.

The *motos* screamed by, almost grazing his body. A pizzeria, a hair salon, a hand-written sign on cardboard above a shop that sold buffalo mozzarella. In Oxford, he'd miss the chaotic vitality of these streets.

He marched up the hill, making good time despite the blast-furnace heat. Suddenly, amid the roar of a scooter, he felt his body tugged; spun around, he was jerked violently and thrown onto the cobblestones, breaking his fall only by landing on the heels of his hands and banging a knee.

"Signor! Signor!" A woman was bent over him. He noticed high-heeled shoes, toes painted a glittery silver against rough cobblestone, and realized that his knapsack was gone.

8

ROBARTS

The Robarts Library at the University of Toronto never looked to Marcus like a library. It was a brutalist fortress evoking brawn over brains. He imagined the librarians defending their books with crossbows and slingshots aimed through arrow-slit windows.

One word had brought him to this citadel of learning, a word which even had a font named after it. *Herculaneum.* Some scholar he'd amounted to! He'd neglected to do the proper research before flying off to Italy. But at least he had that one page of Latin script. A fragment of the puzzle that would help him identify Gerald's scroll if it ever re-materialized. He now desperately wanted the thing back, or at the very least to find out what happened to it. Papyrus scrolls didn't vanish into thin air. It wasn't a Baroque painting that some crime boss could stash away and admire in private, biding his time while its value climbed. This was old paper made of reeds harvested along the Nile.

A few days earlier, he'd photocopied the segment Laszlo had unrolled and sent it to a Latin expert. "Should have done this months ago," Marcus said to himself. There were too many gaps in the text, the Latin too archaic for him to make sense of it. He commissioned the professor to provide a rough translation. In the meantime, he would see what he could dig up in the library about the Herculaneum scrolls.

At a bank of computers, he checked the catalogue, scribbled down some call numbers, made his way to the turnstile, and flashed his library card. On the card, the university's heraldic crest depicted a beaver, three books, and a crown surmounted by a tree. *Velut arbor aevo* was the Latin phrase: "as a tree through the ages." Gerald's scroll yet again came to mind; from the side, its layers were fused like arboreal rings. Yet there had also been a leading edge on the papyrus layers that he could see with a magnifying glass, like on a roll of toilet paper or tape. That leading edge was where the papyrus had been cut by Laszlo after fourteen inches were unrolled on the Piaggio machine.

Marcus took the stairs to get some exercise. It was twelve flights up, better than an elliptical machine. He'd never been a gym person. Tennis was his thing, and he was happy to have recently gone back to the sport. His legs had no issue with the stairs, but he was short of breath long before he made it up. Maybe he should start doing cardio training. Tennis, demanding though it was, required shorter, more explosive bursts of activity.

The library interior had a tough-minded, industrial look that leaned heavily on metal and concrete. Uniform sections of collective desks were affixed with stainless steel reading lamps. Books were relegated to gunmetal shelves located in the dimly lit outskirts of the twelfth floor. Marcus checked the stack directory for call numbers from the Dewey Decimal System, still firmly in place despite the technological changes that had radically transformed the library world. Back when he was a student three decades earlier, learning revolved around actual physical books. These days, gathering knowledge meant consulting databases and digital collections and flash drives. Physical books were a quaint throwback. Librarians *were* being forced to defend their stock.

He sauntered through the stacks, coming to a stop at section PA3339.C7. Marcus loved the tranquility of libraries. Teaching he could live without. But it was a delight to be surrounded by thousands of volumes as a motion sensor triggered light. Suddenly their spines were illuminated.

He scanned the titles, looking for anything related to the Herculaneum scrolls. The gaunt, bearded face of Epicurus on the cover of one hardback was familiar to Marcus from a book Gerald once gave him. *The Art and Science of Ancient Happiness.* Marcus had used it for his course on European intellectual history. Two thousand three hundred years ago, Epicurus had propounded the radical notion that the universe was composed of minuscule, indivisible particles. He saw the physical world as a collision course of random atoms operating in the void. There was no intelligent designer, prime mover, or divine maestro in his philosophy. That would explain Marcus's existence. Sometimes he felt like a seashell adrift, carried along by whatever current happened to be in force. Would nothing ever come along to wash him ashore? Well, Gerald's inheritance had come along. What more could he ask for? Divine intervention?

Epicurus believed in the gods, but with a twist: in his philosophy, Zeus and his Olympian entourage had nothing to do with humans. The gods occupied a perfect realm of tranquility and beauty far removed from the troubles of mere mortals like Marcus. It was a laissez-faire concept of divinity, remarkable for being conceived at a time when the gods were seen as energetically interventionist — turning the tides of battle, disguising themselves to seduce unsuspecting humans, making their presence felt in countless ways.

For Epicurus, death was nothing to worry about — literally "nothing"; humans need not fear the retribution of the gods in any world to come. Armed with this strategy, Epicurus tried to remove the main source of human anxiety. However, Marcus was skeptical that this argument could cure anyone's personal dread of oblivion. Divine wrath didn't trouble him, but fear of death weighed heavy. He'd sometimes focus on the inevitability of death with an intensity that had his heart galloping and breath shallow.

The panic attacks eventually disappeared, but these anxieties were deeply rooted. Before his fifth birthday, his father had suffered a stroke during a tennis match. When he recovered, he walked out on the family. There were letters from South America for a few years, then nothing. Marcus's mother had, for some time, used the Sinclair name for her son. When Marcus was nineteen, she died after a long struggle with lung cancer. Gerald stepped into the vacuum. There was nothing conventional about his uncle; he was no father figure getting home for dinner with a briefcase. He was more often than not out of town. But he had always been a reliable support system. And now Marcus's father figure was gone.

More uplifting was the Epicurean recipe for happiness, which was based on pleasure. The emphasis on pleasure had earned Epicurus an undeserved reputation for loose morals, his name becoming a synonym for wine, women, and song; or, in a more recent era, sex, drugs, and rock 'n' roll. This, Marcus knew, was a distortion of the philosophy, a slur on the bearded Greek for whom tranquility, friendship, and moderate asceticism were the hallmarks of a well-lived life.

The good Epicurean always thinks several moves ahead in order to calculate the net effect of pleasure-seeking. Excessive amounts of booze or food or carousing can bring unhappy consequences, whether the morning after or years down the road. Avoidance of pain was considered as important as pleasure. Perhaps more so, since the absence of pain granted a kind of pleasure in and of itself. The highest pleasure for an Epicurean was freedom from bodily pain and psychological distress — *ataraxia*. That lovely word Gerald had taught Marcus. *A lucid state of robust equanimity.* A fine concept. And who could argue against it being the goal of life?

In the library stacks, he now checked for volumes of *Cronache Ercolanesi*, the Chronicles of Herculaneum, a journal containing the latest research on the papyri. But the section of shelf that normally held the journal was empty, staring back at him with a toothless grin. The journal was probably being repaired or re-catalogued. He had several books in his arms anyway, so he headed to a carrel desk he liked with a southern view of the city, the CN Tower rising in the distance like a massive syringe injecting the sky.

Along the way, he was surprised to see Kristi Grainger at one of the long tables. All those missing volumes of *Cronache Ercolanesi*, some two dozen of them, were stacked on her table. Her eyes were closed, and she was sitting ramrod straight, her hands resting on thighs clad in form-fitting yoga pants. He stopped at an angle across from her, feeling uncomfortably like a peeping Tom. If symmetry accounted for beauty, she'd been well-designed. Her burgundy-streaked dark hair was parted in the middle and tied back in a ponytail, revealing a tall, thoughtful forehead, almond-shaped eyes, a straight nose, and full lips that rounded out the equation.

As if on cue, her eyes opened.

"All roads lead to Herculaneum," he said.

"Oh. Hi."

"Are you okay?"

"Yes. Um . . . I was just meditating."

"Good place for that. How's it going?"

"It's going. My mind is going numb. Not in a good way. From all this stuff." She gestured to the fat volumes of *Cronache Ercolanesi*.

"I know the feeling."

"How so?" Kristi asked. "And what are you doing here?"

"Boning up on the papyrus scrolls. The same as you, I guess."

Their hushed voices were interrupted by her cell phone, a trumpet bursting over trip-hop beats. She declined the call and said, "Let's take a break."

He followed her out of the reading room to a nearby stairwell.

"So," Kristi said, "Google engineer goes to Italy six weeks ago to decode secret scrolls . . ."

"They're not secret."

"They're unreadable," Kristi said. "They're a mystery. Nobody knows what's in most of them. A few have been deciphered, but the rest are impenetrable because of their physical state."

A student took her time climbing up the concrete stairs, and Kristi waited for her to exit the stairwell. "I have some names of people who were in the Officina that day," she said. "A reporter from *Il Mattino*, the Naples newspaper, helped me out. There were several researchers in the area of papyrology." She turned some pages in a spiral-bound notepad, and continued, "Christoph, um, Hirshleifer. Olivier Auger. Lorenzo Clemente. Ring any bells?"

"Auger for sure. I spoke with him a fair bit at the conference. So did Ballard. I don't recognize the other names."

"So Auger was in touch with Ballard?"

"I saw them chatting a few times. Auger is a star papyrologist. Nice guy. He can be quite sardonic and was teasing Ballard about Google being there. But nothing aggressive."

"Sounds like I should talk to him." She leaned onto the metal handrail. "And by the way, you're sure Ballard was not involved romantically with anyone in Naples?"

"I just told you what I saw."

"Or didn't see. For two nights prior to his death, Ballard had a gentleman caller up to his room."

"A gentleman caller?"

"I've been calling the Hotel Greco for days on end, trying to find someone who remembers Ballard and who speaks better English than my Italian. I finally found someone. Spoke to a night manager — apparently they have several. Italy! Anyway, the night manager remembered Ballard because there was a commotion at the front desk one night when a young man arrived to visit Ballard. The man tried to waltz right through the lobby and into an elevator but was intercepted by the front desk. The front desk called Ballard, who had to come down to the lobby and verify that this guy was a friend of his. A friend. At one a.m. Not only that, the same quote-unquote 'friend' showed up again the next night; the night before Ballard was found dead. This time he was allowed to walk straight through." She paused and seemed to want an explanation.

Marcus knew that Ballard had planned to meet with a scientist the day he was killed. He'd told the police in Naples, and now he told Kristi.

"Did you get the name of this visitor?" he asked.

"Not yet. But I will. The night manager said he'd check the front desk visitor records. He's off for a couple of days."

A fluorescent tube light overhead cast an eerie, orangey glow. A sign in bold red letters said, *NOT An Emergency Stairwell*.

"I guess I misread Ballard," Marcus said. "But who knows? I mean, who ever knows about these things from the outside? Ballard just didn't come across like the sort of guy who was up to late-night dalliances. Of whatever sort."

"You'd be surprised what goes on behind closed doors."

"Closed hotel doors, especially, I guess."

She smiled, but not her usual business-like smile, a different smile, he thought: a smile with something behind it. He wondered whether it was projection on his part. Or did she in fact open a door ever so slightly to reveal something softer and more playful?

9

NAPLES

Her new office was a major disappointment when Carmela Zuccarello was promoted to the post of homicide squad police chief. The promise that she'd be moved to a renovated wing of the building languished in the bureaucratic ether. For the foreseeable future, and quite possibly for the rest of her career, Zuccarello expected to be confined to a cramped space with nothing to see out the window but the bricks of the adjacent building. Difficult to imagine that just outside was the vibrant pedestrian walkway of Via Toledo and, on the other side, the sparkling Bay of Naples. A dreary office, she told herself, at least enabled better focus on work.

The absence of a scenic view also justified her collection of snow globes neatly arrayed on a shelf. She was focusing on the snow globe of Rome, the Colosseum taking up most of the scene. None of these souvenirs offered very original takes on their cities: Empire State Building, Golden Gate Bridge, Eiffel Tower, and so on. Kitschy, for sure. But there was something soothing about them, something that took her out of her own bubble.

The Trevor Ballard case, uppermost in her mind, was a head-scratcher. The partial autopsy report was in. No sign of struggle. No blows to the body. No evidence of cancer, stroke, or cardiovascular disease. She awaited the complete autopsy report as well as toxicology and blood work. But she had no doubt that someone had killed Ballard. His missing computer and cell phone said as much. Not to mention the two pairs of nitrile gloves in the waste bin. And there was blood, presumably coughed up by Ballard himself, that vivid red splattered in the hotel room sink.

There were so many shades of red in Naples. When Zuccarello was an art history student, she prided herself on identifying the different hues: dusty rose, burnt ochre, terracotta, and that Pompeian red, originally monochrome yellow but turned to red when the volcano transformed the pigment's chemistry. The red in Ballard's bathroom sink was straight-forward crimson, as brilliant as paint squeezed straight from the tube.

She'd, of course, been careful not to contaminate the crime scene, which she entered wearing gloves and paper shoes. Then the National Scientific Police, the CSI team, took control of the scene, taping off the hotel room, dusting for fingerprints and conducting presumptive blood tests. A local coroner was admitted to confirm the fact of death.

Grunt work on the case had been assigned to Giuseppe, who con-tinued to whine about their breakup. To her surprise, the procrastinator in all matters save for his sex drive had made actual headway with Google. Giuseppe learned that Ballard had no longer been employed by the tech giant. A parallel company of Ballard's own creation had produced some sort of conflict of interest. The details of his terminated contract with Google were confidential, but apparently he had left the company two months prior to his death.

A senior engineer at a behemoth like Google must have accumu-lated enemies. A parallel company, conflict of interest, confidential termination — all these factors pointed to friction, animosity, power struggles. But all that had taken place far away in California, not in Campania. Although, if you wanted to dispose of someone far from home . . .

She thought of the American expat, Sweeney. He was also a Californian. And she remembered that piece of mail she'd seen at his home, PurplePapyrus. She would put Giuseppe on that.

Meanwhile, she had other pressing matters to address. A magistrate blown to pieces in Torre del Greco when a hit man attached a bomb to the car door at a red light. At a wedding reception in Portici, a waiter was fatally stabbed by a guest. But neither of these puzzled her as much as the death of an American software engineer attending a conference about papyrus scrolls.

She removed one of her snow globes from the shelf. San Francisco, close enough to where Mr. Trevor Ballard had lived. The city, which she'd visited once when living in the United States, was impressively compressed in its little dome. If only Naples could be so neatly encapsulated.

She gave the memento a shake, and a blizzard of snowflakes filled the minuscule city like tiny shreds of evidence, a paper trail scattered in the air.

10

MIDTOWN

It was hard for Marcus not to think of Gerald while living in a condo that gave so many reminders of its longtime owner. The living room alone, the *salon*, as Gerald called it, featured Roman busts, Greek vases, an urn with snake handles, and a larger-than-life pockmarked marble torso. A fragment of a Roman mosaic decorated one wall; two other walls were lined with carved wooden shelves filled with art books. What looked like a very old door lay flat on four marble Ionic columns and served as a coffee table.

An oil painting that felt out of place amid the antiquities showed the cityscape of Budapest, where Gerald Aldabert Szarkas had been born in 1928. His father had been a Roman Catholic art dealer; his Jewish mother an accomplished pianist.

Marcus knew well the turbulent family saga. Hungarian Jews had managed to avoid deportation until 1944, when Gerald and his sister Katharina fled the Nazis by getting a seat at the last minute on the so-called "Kastner Train." They were among a thousand Jews who made the harrowing journey from Budapest through Austria and Germany, running the terrifying gauntlet of Nazi checkpoints to safety in Switzerland. Their mother would perish in Auschwitz; their father survived the war years but hanged himself not long afterwards. Gerald had recounted more than once how his father supplied him with resources for bribes. Gold, jewelry, gems, and cash "saved *our* lives," he said, "but not his." Gerald looked after his younger sister until three years after the war when they were sent to live with a cousin in Canada. He anglicized the family name to Sinclair, earned a master's degree in art history at the University of Toronto, and launched his career dealing antiquities.

Marcus, an only child, grew up hearing about his Uncle Gerald's rakishness and skirt-chasing. The stories were difficult to square with the gentle, pipe-smoking man he knew when he was a small child. But a few years later, Gerald would pick his nephew up from school occasionally, showing up in a sleek Jaguar. He'd place the grade-schooler in the backseat and toggle between the gas and brakes for a thrilling joyride. As Marcus got older, Gerald advised him on sports, then girls, then his career. And now Marcus had inherited Gerald's substantial estate and was living in his townhouse.

A few days after crossing paths with Kristi in the library, Marcus was jolted awake at an ungodly hour by a bad dream. In the dream, he was clutching a scroll while falling into a kaleidoscope of dazzling triangles and multi-coloured arrows. With an intense burst of anger, he hurled the scroll to the ground, where it shattered into pieces. He could just make out Latin letters he strained to read before waking up, his long hair matted and sweaty on his face. He threw on clothes from the previous day — his usual dress code of T-shirt, jeans, and running shoes — and dragged his sleep-deprived body to the kitchen.

The feeling of anger in the dream felt distant but not entirely foreign. He'd wrestled with it early in life. He wondered: What became of that rage that coursed through his veins as a teenager? It had been directed at his parents, teachers, authority figures, and then vanished. He remembered youthful fistfights, gasping for air, hyperventilating, a panic attack repurposed. And that was before a single punch landed. Eventually he'd purchased boxing gloves and sparred with friends in basements clouded with pot smoke where it felt as if mostly brain cells were getting pummelled. Under the influence of Bruce Lee movies, he studied karate but was bored after umpteen sessions on how to fall correctly. He even learned how to use nunchucks, the Japanese martial arts weapons, and sewed a pocket into the inside of his jean jacket to carry them. How far away that all felt now. Where did all that anger go? It just folded its tent and left.

While grinding coffee beans in Gerald's espresso machine, he recalled an academic article about dreams, one of many digressions in his Herculaneum readings. Most people in antiquity, the Stoics included, believed dreams could be directly sent by the gods and therefore could predict the future. The Epicureans dismissed that idea, considering dreams to be purely biological phenomena. He'd done a stint in therapy and had his own theory, more Freud than Jung, rejecting the fashionable idea that dreams were a meaningless clearinghouse of daily detritus.

What would a therapist have to say about his obsession — and was it really an obsession, or just a *preoccupation* — with Gerald's scroll? Was the attachment merely symbolic? He thought not. It struck him as perfectly reasonable. He had to track down the scroll. The segment Laszlo had unrolled was ample proof that the scroll once belonged to him. The text was beguiling. But Google Translate had gotten nowhere. A papyrologist was needed to make full sense of the text, but there weren't many around. Marcus had read that there were only some five hundred in the world, and not all of them knew Latin. An even smaller slice of those experts could deal with a damaged Herculaneum scroll. For the time being, an expert in Latin literature would have to suffice. In a few days, Marcus would be meeting the professor he'd hired to translate the segment of the scroll unrolled by Laszlo.

The coffee beans ricocheted in the hopper of the machine, triggering a memory of Ballard. The engineer was fond of his coffee, so much so that he'd brought a portable bean grinder to Naples. One afternoon, during a break in the conference, Ballard had even made Marcus an americano in his hotel room. Bringing DIY coffee paraphernalia to Italy, the land of sublime *crema*, was a coals-to-Newcastle move. And here was a computer engineer smitten with an old-school crank mechanism that was about as high-tech as an eighteenth-century Piaggio machine.

The Piaggio machine had worked well. Until it didn't. And Ballard had been alive and well. Until he wasn't.

Marcus's days at Gerald's condo began with his uncle's home-delivered *Financial Times* and breakfast in a kitchen with marble floor tiles, which remained pleasantly cool to his bare feet, though with a tinge of sadness. Gerald's tennis partners, invariably younger than him, had worried that the old man risked serious injury on the clay court. Marcus, who occasionally (and gently) hit balls with his uncle, shared that concern. Yet what had done him in was a nocturnal fall on his bathroom's marble floor. Marble being an ironic end for an antiquities dealer.

On this day, as on so many recently, Marcus set out for the Robarts Library. He didn't have much else to do now that he was no longer teaching. The walk to the library took fifteen minutes and was not without charm. He passed immaculate Victorian and Gothic homes that might have been made of gingerbread, then a stretch of art galleries, boutique investment houses, and a real estate firm curiously named Virtue. Not the sort of virtue that was the main goal of ancient Stoicism.

As he passed the Royal Ontario Museum, its modern glass and aluminum addition looking like the aftermath of a traffic smashup, he thought of Kristi. She'd written that series of articles about the ROM. Lately, whenever he ventured into the library stacks, all the volumes of *Cronache Ercolanesi* were snugly in place; no journalist with burgundy streaks in her hair was leaning intensely over a mess of books and periodicals. No surprise that he found himself wanting to cross paths with her again. Her looks and smarts and *carpe diem*ism were irresistible.

From Bloor, he turned south and entered Philosopher's Walk, a leafy sanctuary at the University of Toronto campus shaded by willow, oak, and beech trees. Cast-iron benches were affixed with little memorial plaques that quoted from the likes of Rumi, Jane Austen, and a self-described "Philosophical Adviser to the Galaxy" who had declared, "*L'essentiel est invisible pour les yeux.*"

Marcus had many memories of this idyllic enclave from his student days. Relationships had formed, and in one case ended, under these beautiful trees. Those years were a mixed experience for him. Sadly, he never mustered the wherewithal to finish his Ph.D. dissertation on the French medieval historian Marc Bloch, who became an anti-Nazi resistance fighter.

Emerging from the walkway, Marcus could see the periscope-like tower of the Robarts Library rising in the west. Blink, and it could be one of the many construction cranes framing the skies of the city. Soon he was inside the library, at a reading table piled with books and journals about the Herculaneum scrolls. He began with the history of their decipherment. He already knew the story of Father Piaggio. After two years of unrolling on his machine, Piaggio reached the end of that first scroll, where the author's name was finally revealed. Not a Sophocles or a Livy, but an obscure Epicurean philosopher writing about music: Philodemus. The next scroll opened was also by this Philodemus. And the next one after that.

Philodemus was the in-house philosopher for a wealthy Roman statesman, Lucius Calpurnius Piso Caesoninus, known as Piso. Caesoninus! Was that the "Caes" name that had become indistinct in Gerald's scroll due to the wear and tear of the papyrus?

Marcus delved into the history of Piso Caesoninus, who had owned the Villa dei Papiri. There seemed to be precious little biographical material about the man and scant trace of his existence. What little survived the ancient world was often random, a product of happenstance. A case in point were the scrolls from Herculaneum, which only survived because they were carbonized by a volcanic eruption and discovered by chance seventeen centuries later.

Blind *fortuna*. A swerve of atoms.

Not much more was known about Philodemus. He was born around 110 BC in Gadara, in modern-day Jordan. As a young man, he made his way to Athens and then travelled to Alexandria, Egypt, Sicily, and finally to Naples. There he acquired his influential Roman patron, Piso.

As Marcus dipped into the writings of Philodemus, he felt as if he were reading two very different authors. The philosophical works were ponderous, mechanical, and rigidly governed by Epicurean philosophy. Yet in verse, Philodemus was sensitive, playful, and lascivious. His love poetry jumped off the page. Some of the names and references were obscure, forcing Marcus to consult the explanatory notes. But the gist of it was clever and clear enough.

> Philaeniŏn is short and dark;
> her hair is more curly than parsley,
> her skin is more tender than down;
> her voice holds more magic
> than the girdle of Aphrodite;
> she refuses me nothing
> and asks nothing in return.
> Such a Philaeniŏn grant me,
> golden Aphrodite, to love,
> until I find another more perfect.

He felt a tap on his shoulder.

"I have some news."

Kristi was using her library voice and tilted her head, signalling him to leave the reading room. He turned his book on its face and followed her with some bounce in his step to a glassed-in chamber, presumably soundproof, that was meant to be used by study groups.

"I was wrong," she said.

"Wrong about what?"

"Wrong about Ballard. The mystery gentleman caller. It was nothing sexual. There was a visitor. But he was there on business."

"That makes more sense to me. What kind of business?"

"Tech. The late-night visitor was an Italian physicist named Cipressi, working for a technology firm called Napolimage."

"That fits with what Ballard told me. A 'scientist.' But it was supposed to be a lunch."

Kristi said, "Who knows? There are lots of experts in this field. I spoke with the guy. His English is decent. Says that someone passed Ballard's coordinates onto him, he got in touch and had two meetings with Ballard in his hotel room. Sounds totally legit."

"Imaging technology. For the scrolls."

"Indeed."

"And did anything come of it?"

"Not that I can see. The physicist says that Ballard wanted to combine some newfangled Google software with the imaging hardware that his firm had access to. Scanning equipment of the kind used for subatomic particle-smashing or something. Ballard wanted to do a test case on a scroll."

Marcus's heart jumped.

A librarian retrieved a cart that held books, glanced at the two non-students chatting in the glass-walled room, and wheeled the cart away.

"A scroll. Did he say *which* scroll?"

"No," Kristi said. "We're supposed to speak again tomorrow."

"Well done! How did you get to him?"

"The hotel gave me his name. I also scoured the discussion groups for Herculaneum and papyrus scrolls and papyrology, and his name came up there as well. He says he knows only about the technology end of things but is happy to share what he knows."

A gaggle of students emerged from the nearby elevator with phones, earbuds, computers, gym bags, and no books in evidence.

Marcus said, "Any chance I might listen in on that next conversation?"

"I'm afraid not. Why?"

"Maybe he can help me track down my uncle's scroll. I mean, he's from Naples. And he obviously knows something about these scrolls."

"I'm sorry. I don't do interviews with someone else sitting in. That's not the way journalism works."

"But what if I had something to offer in return? An interview of my own?"

"Meaning what?"

"You know that segment of Gerald's scroll unrolled by Laszlo? I've arranged to have it properly translated. By an academic who knows her way around a papyrus. You might want to sit in on that discussion."

11

THE ANNEX

In a journalism career that spanned three decades, Kristi Grainger had occupied a front-row seat for every transgression worth a headline, from grisly murder to environmental destruction, white-collar crime to political malfeasance.

She was also well acquainted with the debate surrounding looted antiquities. Kristi had written those in-depth articles for the *Star* (back when the paper had the resources to underwrite in-depth articles) about artifacts that the Royal Ontario Museum had acquired from a dealer suspected of smuggling. The more she reported, the more new tips came in, leading to yet more investigative stories.

She knew that every rich country displayed foreign plunder. The "Elgin" marbles were taken from the Parthenon in Athens and the Treasury of Atreus in Mycenae to sit in the British Museum. The Rosetta stone was there as well, despite repeated calls for its return to Egypt. The same museum had some of the Benin bronzes; thousands of these precious objects stolen from what is now Nigeria are spread across the globe.

Herculaneum was no exception. The first person to pull antiquities out of the ground there was a French aristocrat working for the Austrian empire. He had shipped the female portrait statues known as the "Herculaneum Women" to Vienna; they were now on display in Dresden, Germany. Italy, a victim of so much looting, had itself grabbed plenty of antiquities from Greece and other countries and refused to relinquish them. A case in point was a marble statue of Venus that Italian soldiers had stolen in Libya a century ago.

But there were grey areas in the debate. Dealers, perhaps like Marcus's uncle, argued that had people like them not purchased artifacts, tomb raiders would simply have sold them to criminals. Invaluable antiquities would have been melted down or simply gone missing. Because they bought art, it was preserved. Kristi herself had seen and appreciated the fabulous wall paintings from the Boscoreale villa, also buried by Mount Vesuvius, at the Metropolitan Museum in New York.

Yet the world had changed and no longer tolerated the indiscriminate looting typical of previous centuries. A UNESCO convention stipulated the return of cultural property illicitly exported. Italy had a law — passed by Benito Mussolini — protecting its own cultural treasures; antiquities could not be exported without a license. So even if Gerald Sinclair had bought the scroll from someone who'd acquired it after 1939, when the Italian antiquities law was passed, he'd still have needed the paperwork to show provenance. She dug into her files for information about Sinclair, the antiquities dealer. Nothing there. He presumably wasn't a big enough fish.

Kristi had no patience for unethical behaviour. How to live life could be boiled down to three words: do no harm. Eight letters; that was it. Aside from the big-picture issues, she could get worked up over petty annoyances: bad music on phone holds; people taking forever at the cash to buy lottery tickets; motorists refusing to signal. The list was endless. Thankfully, her meditation practice was making her more tolerant.

So she didn't blow up when Marcus requested to join her interview with the Italian "scientist" who'd been Ballard's late-night visitor. Marcus simply didn't understand how journalists functioned; having a non-reporter tag along for an interview was a non-starter.

AN INTERNET SEARCH SHOWED that the visitor to Ballard's hotel room, Antonio Cipressi, held a Ph.D. in theoretical physics from the University of Padova, had obtained several post-doctoral positions, and conducted research at the European Synchrotron Radiation Facility in Grenoble, France. His Facebook profile showed a chubby, round-faced man with blue-framed glasses and a trim goatee.

The day after bumping into Marcus at the library, Kristi dialed Cipressi's number. The high-pitched, cheerful voice familiar from their previous call came on the line. After some small talk about the sweltering weather in Naples, Kristi asked Cipressi how it was that he came to know Ballard.

"He sent me an email. He had heard about the technology I had been experimenting with. Virtual unwrapping technique on items like papyri. It's no secret. He had similar ideas related to Google's book-scanning software. He wanted to compare expertise."

"Interesting. Can you tell me, roughly, in layman's terms, how the technique would work?"

"I cannot talk about details. But in general, yes. The concept has two stages. First a scroll is scanned in a synchrotron. You have to get beam time somewhere, which is not easy. Then you use computer software and machine-learning on the high-res 3-D scans."

Kristi said, "And have you actually done this?"

"No. It is not so easy as it sounds."

"I can imagine," said Kristi. "And what about Ballard? Do you have any idea why anyone would want to murder him?"

"It is so sad about Trevor. He was so excited. 'I will undress a scroll with my eyes,' he said. I can't believe he is dead. I have no idea who would want to kill him. Do you have theories?"

"I was hoping you might have one," Kristi said. "Or help me figure it out."

"The story is not so rational, like the cosmos has no meaning. I know only that he was meeting with many people in Naples. And even women, you know what I mean?"

"Um, not really. You mean he was dating women in Italy?"

"Something like that. He was telling me about his 'polyamorous' life. That's the word he used. He was asking me where he could meet women. I told him about a bar in Naples. That's the only suggestion I had for him."

"I see. You suggested he go to a bar to meet women?"

"Jungle Bar. In Alabardieri."

"And do you know if he went there?"

"I don't know. He seemed to like the idea. It was already late when I left the hotel. He also went out. I don't know where. I never got to ask him. The next day he was dead."

JUNGLE BAR. It sounded like a club that would fit right into Kristi's part of town. The day after her interview with Cipressi, Kristi was walking in her Annex neighbourhood and musing about what he had said about Trevor Ballard being polyamorous. Ballard would have found a welcome somewhere in her hood, which had a fair number of students, artists, and hipsters.

Was Marcus so clued out that he had no such inkling about Ballard? So it seemed. Marcus was the kind of guy who needed a flashing neon sign to get the message, the sort of sign you found outside a club called Jungle Bar. Perhaps it was a case of having blinders on, so obsessed he seemed to be with that stolen scroll. Did he even realize how risky it might be to try to track it down? He seemed to think that he could just waltz back into Naples, the *jungle* of Naples, and retrieve the thing. They may not kill foreign journalists in Naples, but Google engineers were apparently fair game. A retired teacher trying to find a blood-soaked treasure would be well advised to watch his step.

She passed her usual haunts on College Street, the second-hand bookstore that employed Scrabble tiles as genre labels on its shelves: not exactly the Dewey Decimal System, but way more fun. The Hogtown Vegan, Starving Artist Waffles, and of course, Bar Raval, that curvaceous watering hole that could have been designed by Gaudí.

A streetcar swooshed by, reminding her of how Gaudí died — hit by a tram in Barcelona with no identification papers on him, the great architect of La Sagrada Familia later dying in hospital like another anonymous street person. Kristi had been to wondrous Barcelona, but it had been ages since she'd been anywhere far away, and she was more than ready to travel again. Italy would do fine, and it seemed like she would have to go there in pursuit of her story.

A huge man draped in billowy black clothes was walking an incredibly tiny dog. Behind him was a woman whose T-shirt read, *Jesus is not a weekend thing*. A car alarm went off. Two men wearing yellow hard hats and matching reflector vests looked her way. To discourage their interest, she checked her phone. No new messages relating to the story she was working on. She wished she had an idea what Trevor Ballard had been up to. She had plenty more research to do, starting with Ballard's extracurricular activities. And of course, the papyrus scroll. Why anyone would get rolled for such an obscure artifact was beyond her. Yet Marcus seemed convinced that was the motivation behind the murder.

Where was Marcus, anyway? He was supposed to be waiting for her at the corner of College and Augusta.

12

WATERLOO

Among the items Marcus had inherited from Gerald was a classic car in mint condition. The slate-grey Jaguar XJ6 represented state-of-the-art luxury, circa 1996. Tan interior with real wood accents. Comfy seats, though the suspension had seen better days.

He finally had a reason to get behind the wheel. The professor he'd hired to translate that section of the scroll Laszlo had unrolled was ready to give him a rough summary of the contents in person. She taught in southwestern Ontario at the University of Waterloo, just one hour's drive away in the old Jag.

Marcus had mentioned the meeting to Kristi, hoping she'd give him access to the Italian physicist in exchange for coming with him today. No dice. But he invited her to tag along anyway. And there she was, on the corner of College and Augusta.

"Cool — there's even a tape deck," said Kristi after she hopped in the car.

"And I have some old tapes," Marcus said. "Nineties tunes to go with the car's vintage."

"Such as?" Kristi wanted to know.

"Let's see. Beck. Pavement. Björk."

"Good choices. What else?"

"There's a bunch of stuff. Prince. Alanis. Liz Phair. Take your pick."

An hour later, after motoring to propulsive songs like "Everyday is a Winding Road," they reached Waterloo. The university campus did not feature the usual vine-clad, weathered brick buildings. Instead, they oohed and aahed over the futuristic nanotechnology and quantum computing buildings.

Marcus said, "Imagine the heated discussions that go on in there about subatomic equations!"

The type of equations, he mused, that calculated how fourteen-odd billion years ago, the entire cosmos was contained in a minuscule singularity. The whole shebang supposedly began with quantum fluctuations in the void, microscopic particles coming together and then, some ten billion years later, natural selection on planet Earth, all leading to — to what? To this particular moment with an attractive journalist in his late uncle's sedan? Life was therefore a random process that just happened to produce Marcus and his consciousness?

I don't buy that, he thought. *Everything about the Big Bang, sure, but my* mind — *not that it's anything special as far as minds go* — *but consciousness as just some freak hiccup of nature?* His consciousness couldn't be nothing more than a meaningless side effect of evolution that would fade away as surely as it came into existence. Or could it?

"Are you lost, or what?"

Marcus steered the Jaguar toward one of the older buildings on campus. Soon they were sitting in the cramped office belonging to Margaret Pasternak, director of the Waterloo Institute for Hellenistic Studies.

"As agreed," Pasternak said, "I won't provide you with a literal, word-for-word translation. But I can give you a rough sketch of what's here."

"Great," Marcus said. "We're all ears."

"So what we have here is basically an imaginary correspondence between Julius Caesar and his father-in-law. It's designed to look like one single letter from a collection of correspondence that an affluent Roman aristocrat might well have compiled. The letter here, the first columns at any rate, indicate that it's addressed to Lucius Calpurnius Piso Caesoninus. The text, as you can see, ends abruptly before the letter concludes. It's simply cut off, truncated. But it's obvious what it's supposed to be: a letter written to Piso by Julius Caesar."

Marcus's heart skipped a beat, and he shot a glance at Kristi, but she stayed focused on the professor. Pasternak was summarizing the first segment that Laszlo had unrolled before the papyrus tore. The missing conclusion of the letter was still on the scroll itself, wherever that was.

"It's a very good fake, actually," Pasternak said. "Your uncle obviously had some scholarly training and studied Caesar in depth."

Marcus had told her that the text he'd transcribed and mailed to her was concocted by his late uncle, who dabbled in classical studies.

Pasternak continued, "It is apparently written in the preclassical capital script, which dates the writing to the latter part of the first century BC. It even has lacunae, gaps in the text, which suggests your uncle was going for the authenticity of a damaged papyrus scroll. I'm frankly surprised such an arcane creation even exists. Which raises another point I wanted to make: just so you know, I will obviously not be party to any forgery attempt."

"Oh, not at all," Marcus said. "There's no way I would attempt such a thing. Nor would Gerald . . . my uncle. Gerald Sinclair."

"Well, whatever his motivation, your uncle evidently had some knowledge in this department," Pasternak said.

"He was brilliant," Marcus said. "A remarkable man."

"Clearly, because he did an excellent job writing this. So I'll have to assume he was just indulging in a private hobby and not trying to make money by faking a priceless artifact."

"Correct," said Marcus, trying to be as truthful as he could. "He left this document to me in his will. He never tried to sell it."

"All right, then. So, as I was saying, this letter is addressed to Piso. He came from an aristocratic family. He was at one time a Roman consul, which was the highest post in the government of the Republic. And most famously, he was the father-in-law of Caesar. His daughter Calpurnia was Caesar's third wife."

Kristi finally looked at Marcus; clearly, they had the same thought. Pasternak considered this to be an impressive imitation of a letter from Julius Caesar — which meant the text was *in fact* a letter from Julius Caesar!

Julius Caesar!

"Interesting," Marcus said. He was gobsmacked but trying not to show it. "Can I just ask why you say the text is obviously a made-up letter and not the real thing? What did my uncle do that gives it away?"

"Well, it's *obvious!*" Pasternak said, removing her tortoiseshell glasses from her nose and letting them dangle from a cord around her neck. Her superior manner hit a nerve: Marcus had never finished his Ph.D.; he'd been a community college teacher and not a university prof. He'd been subjected to such academic condescension more than once before.

"For starters," she continued, "Caesar's correspondence has not survived, to our knowledge, on papyri. Of course, papyrus is an organic material which decomposes after a few centuries. Some letters were written on wax tablets or thin plates of wood. Nothing to speak of has survived in that form either. But only a small percentage of works on papyri has survived the period. That's par for the course for all of antiquity."

"Understood," said Marcus. "So what does the letter go on to say?"

Pasternak fussily adjusted her glasses, tapped her keyboard, and read from the screen. "So, what we have here is Caesar informing Piso that he — Caesar — is planning to legally adopt his child by Cleopatra, Caesarion, who at this period would have been a young boy."

Marcus felt a jolt of nerves, astounded by what he just heard, and looked at Kristi, who was writing rapidly in her spiral notepad.

"Okay, hypothetically speaking," Marcus said, "would that have been possible? Could such a letter have actually been written?"

"Caesar's actual will designated as heir his great-nephew, a teenager named Octavian, who would go on to become Augustus, the first Roman emperor. That was a major shock at the time, revealed only after Caesar's assassination. But there is evidence that Caesar revised his will at least once. Could he have done it again? It's possible."

Kristi glanced up from her notebook at the professor, who'd paused to take a breath.

Pasternak continued, "However, designating as heir his child with someone who was not a Roman citizen — Cleopatra — would have been problematic, to say the least. It would not conform to Roman law. But Caesar was very capable of bending the law to his will. So the short answer is yes, it's possible that Caesar could have written such a letter. But it would have turned history on its head."

"How so?" Marcus asked.

"Oh, you name it. The whole Roman Empire, which followed Caesar's death, was the creation of Octavian, who, as I said, became Augustus, the first Roman emperor. The empire delineated the future borders of Europe and beyond in ways that we are still living with today. Future wars proceeded according to these borders. In addition, Christianity's success was the product of a later Roman emperor. We can point to any number of major world events that came to pass because of the empire. And had Caesar adopted Caesarion instead of Octavian-Augustus as his son, *none* of this would have unfolded in quite the same way."

"We would have had Emperor Caesarion instead?" Kristi asked.

"Well, who can say? Certainly it would have been an uphill battle for young Caesarion. You know, he was murdered on Octavian's orders while fleeing Egypt after Antony and Cleopatra were defeated. Octavian saw Caesarion as a genuine threat."

A truck was beeping somewhere in the distance, but Marcus barely heard it. He realized that despite her initial haughtiness, Pasternak was speaking with passion about a topic she genuinely cared about.

"After all," she continued, "Caesarion was the son of Julius Caesar, who traced his lineage back to the founder of Rome and who was designated an actual god after his assassination, as well as being the son of Cleopatra, who came from the most royal of royal houses, tracing her lineage back to one of Alexander the Great's bodyguards, Ptolemy I Soter, who succeeded Alexander. She was also worshipped as a goddess of the sky, Isis. So both of Caesarion's parents were considered to be deities." She arched an eyebrow to mock that notion.

"Holy crap!" said Kristi. "History could have turned out so differently."

"One can speculate until the cows come home," Pasternak said.

Marcus said, "Speculate away. I have a soft spot for the what-ifs of alternative history."

"What if," she repeated, picking up a ballpoint pen and pressing it to her chin. "Okay. What if Caesarion took power and solidified in a far more organic way the eastern and western parts of the empire? He would have spoken Greek and Egyptian like his mother and Latin like his father. And maybe, just maybe, the massive chasm between the east and west of the Empire, which came about a few centuries later, would have been avoided. Sort of like what Alexander the Great had tried to accomplish. A fusion of geography and cultures. Caesarion instead of Octavian at the head of that empire would have been less Italian, with a more 'Eastern' centre of gravity. Rather than East against West, a conflict which I dare say," she dangled her glasses again and raised that eyebrow, "continues to plague us today."

The wheels in Marcus's head were spinning with the implications of what he'd just heard. If his scroll comprised actual correspondence with Julius Caesar, it was living up to the hype that Herculaneum enthusiasts were forever trumpeting.

He asked Pasternak: "So, if Caesar actually wrote Piso asking for his will to be changed, why might it never have happened?"

"You mean hypothetically?"

"Yes, hypothetically."

"Well, think about it." She removed her reading glasses and fiddled with them. "Piso's daughter Calpurnia was Caesar's wife. I'm not sure Piso would have wanted to help legitimize Caesar's out-of-wedlock child with a foreign woman. Moreover, Piso was a stalwart Roman grandee. An ex-consul whose forebears were consuls going back generations. Blue, blue blood. He would not have been keen to rock the boat that was Republican Rome. *Dignitas* and all the traditional Roman values of integrity and family. Given the presumed date of the letter — ostensibly written from Munda, where a famous battle took place — about one year after its composition, Caesar was killed, and all hell broke loose in the Roman Republic. The masses were seething mad that their hero had been murdered."

"He really was their hero, wasn't he?" Kristi asked.

"Oh, very much so. He was a populist of the first order," Pasternak said. Her voice had taken on a wistful tone, as if she were recalling an old memory.

"At any rate, a civil war began brewing between Caesar's loyalists, like Mark Antony and Piso, pitting them against the men who assassinated him. When Caesar was killed, Cleopatra was actually in Rome, where Caesar had put her up at his own mansion near Janiculum Hill. With her royal entourage and her infant son, Caesar's son. She saw which way the wind was blowing; she hightailed it back to Alexandria along with her son. It is hard to imagine that Piso would further inflame the turbulent political situation by pushing for Cleopatra's son Caesarion to inherit Caesar's estate. Especially since he would disgrace his daughter Calpurnia in the process."

Marcus realized his leg was pumping, his right shoe operating an invisible kick drum. "Okay, assuming all this," he said, "*hypo-thetically*."

He dragged that word out. "How could Caesar have thought he could pull this off? Because you make it sound like a non-starter from the get-go."

"Nothing was a non-starter with Julius Caesar!" she said. "Let me put on my hypothetical hat."

Was she mocking his mockery of the word "hypothetical"? As if it were unscholarly? He should have told her he had many years of teaching history under his belt. But stick to the subject at hand. Keep his ego out of it. It was her brain he was picking.

She continued, "Caesar had recently forced the Senate to designate him Dictator for Life. He had no legitimate children. Well, he once had a daughter, Julia, from his first wife; a beloved daughter, but she had died seven years earlier. So he's childless. A dictator for life, quite possibly desiring kingship, which was a red flag for Romans, breaking every taboo in the book. He's verging on divine status in some circles, particularly in the East. And he happens to have one actual flesh-and-blood child, a son, by Cleopatra, whose own political legitimacy goes back to Alexander the Great. And Egypt being a fabulously rich country that Rome needs for its supplies and expansionary designs going forward. So would making Caesarion his heir have been a non-starter? Maybe. Maybe not.

"Oh," Pasternak added. "There's another fact from the historical record that conceivably supports the theory this letter suggests." She adjusted her glasses again and scanned the screen. "Caesar had asked a senator, Lucius Cornelius Cinna, to pass legislation in the Senate which would allow him to take more than one wife for the purpose of legally begetting a child."

"Seriously?" Kristi asked.

"Seriously."

"*Plus ça change*," Kristi added. "I can't say I'm as impressed with Caesar as you guys seem to be."

Pasternak produced a smile. "Well, be that as it may, your uncle did his homework," she said. "This is a very clever work. Surprisingly clever. If there was any correspondence between Caesar and Piso, his father-in-law, it would surely have been kept in the Villa dei Papiri, which was owned by Piso. And we know that some documents stored there survived because of the eruption of Mount Vesuvius that . . ."

She paused, distracted by a digital chirp, and checked her cell phone. "Excuse me for the interruption. Where was I?"

"You were saying that whoever wrote this dotted their i's and crossed their t's."

"Exactly. It's very well done. By the way, do you know what your uncle intended to do with this?"

"That's a good question," Marcus said.

He looked at Kristi as if for an answer. She didn't have one.

"My uncle's papers are in disarray. I'm hoping that your translation here will help me put this item in the proper file. I'm just trying to put everything in order. And if I can understand something about his, his little hobby here, then so much the better."

"Your uncle sounds like a very interesting man," Pasternak said. "And it's interesting that he wrote something creative about Julius Caesar's will and its implications for Caesar's own grand-nephew, Octavian, and now you — your uncle's nephew — are putting his own papers in order."

"Hmmm. I hadn't made that connection," Marcus said.

"And just so you know," Pasternak added, "Caesar was Octavian's source of power. And Caesar's downfall was a fate his heir always had to keep in mind."

That comment seemed to come out of left field to Marcus. "Point taken," he said.

Kristi said, "I guess it's never easy inheriting an empire."

13

NAPLES

The National Archaeological Museum evoked mixed feelings in David Brill. The vast majority of the treasures hauled out of the ground at Herculaneum and Pompeii were housed there. Scrape away a bit of hardened mud or pumice, handle with care, and there they were: bronze, marble, or mosaic — unearthed, comprehensible, and beautiful.

He was envious, in a way. The unveiling of a carbonized papyrus was more problematic. And yet problem-solving was precisely what drew him to the scrolls.

Brill stopped outside the massive building, admiring the peach-coloured facade accented by grey pediments. As he climbed steps framed by Corinthian columns, he removed his straw hat and carefully tied its chinstrap to his knapsack. Since the motorbike mugging, he'd been using a new knapsack that didn't feel quite right.

He flashed his membership card, passing through the turnstile and into the entranceway where a marble Atlas strained beneath the weight of the world. A copy, like so much Roman art, of the Greek original. And like so much Greek art, the original was lost, and a Roman knock-off from the second century AD was now the next best thing.

The cavernous entrance hall was lined with statues from the Vesuvian towns. Brill noted the dignified presence of M. Nonius Balbus as if he were an old friend. The marble statue of Balbus astride his mount once stood in the Herculaneum theatre. Few museum visitors would know that the original head had gone missing and Balbus had a "modern" head attached to his ancient body.

The opposite of me, mused Brill.

He bounded up the staircase between a pair of reclining Poseidons who seemed to be gossiping to each other: *Did you see who just walked in?*

Brill weaved his way through tourists consulting their phones and guidebooks, pausing to catch his breath on the first landing before a giant statue of Ferdinand, one of the more ridiculous Bourbon kings who'd ruled Naples. One floor up were the mosaics, wall paintings, and statues from Herculaneum and Pompeii. Brill ventured into a smaller room, away from the crowds, where the story of the papyrus scrolls was illustrated on wall displays.

Two Piaggio machines made of walnut, brass, and glass, standing on carved wooden animal legs, occupied the centre of the room. Roman genius, he thought, expressed itself best not in art but in practical innovations like aqueducts, roads, and arches.

To his surprise, a papyrus scroll was lodged inside one of the machines. Odd that I never noticed this before, he thought. He made out a barely visible catalogue number on the black papyrus, part of it unrolled and stretched like a roll of film. Brill bent down and took a photo with his phone. Had this scroll ever been deciphered? Or even identified? Unlikely. Most of it was still in an unrolled clump at the base of the machine.

"Working on a papyrus, as usual?"

A familiar Italian voice, paved with gravel.

"Gramsci." Brill stood up and shook hands with the bearded man. He was about to mention the scroll lodged in the Piaggio machine but thought better of it; he didn't want to put any ideas into the man's head. Mention the papyrus to Gramsci, and by tomorrow, it might be out of the museum and on the black market.

Gramsci was someone Brill had known in a murky way for many years. He occasionally contacted Brill to act as a consultant. The issue was usually something unprovenanced. Not something Brill approved of — quite the contrary — but so many antiquities had been circulating illegally for so long in Italy that to ignore such trading was to be left out of the loop. Brill could on occasion tip off a university or a museum and at least ensure that some object of value ended up in a reputable place. The Diakopto Fragment, looted from a Greek funeral pyre, was one such example. The world knew more about Pythagoras as a result.

But on this occasion, it was Brill who'd requested the rendezvous.

"Yes, I have been working on a papyrus," he said. He waited for a tourist to press his nose against the glass box encasing the Piaggio machine, snap a photo, and move on.

"For six years, to be precise. It is in the Officina. Philodemus. *On Friendship*, Book Two."

"I'm aware."

"Are you also aware," continued Brill, speaking his very serviceable Italian, "that my heavily notated copy of high-resolution images, my latest research, was contained in a knapsack that was stolen from me in the Spanish Quarter last Wednesday?"

"I'm sorry to hear that," Gramsci said. "The Quartieri Spagnoli can be a dangerous place for knapsacks."

It was hot in the museum, and Gramsci unbuttoned his cuffs, fastidiously rolling them up to his elbow. Brill noticed the tattoo of a rose enveloping the letters PCI, the Communist Party of Italy. He'd seen it before and always found it to be unseemly, more confirmation of dubious dealings.

A gaggle of Japanese tourists trooped through the small room; apparently underwhelmed by the Piaggio machines, they moved on to showier items in the museum.

"I was wondering," said Brill, "whether you might be able to make some inquiries. There was nothing of value in that knapsack to anyone but myself. It represents several years' work. Hard work. I blame myself, of course, for not having transferred all that material onto a hard drive. But the photocopy I was working with was unwieldy, several metres long."

Gramsci checked his phone. "I have a question for you."

"Okay."

"Have you heard anything about a Caesar scroll?" he asked.

"I beg your pardon?"

"What I've heard someone is calling 'the Caesar scroll.'"

"Who's calling it that? There's no 'Caesar scroll.'"

"Excuse me. I must have misinterpreted what I heard. But I will see what I can do about your knapsack, professor. I make no promises, obviously. I will let you know."

With that, Gramsci glanced at his phone again, gave Brill an affectionate squeeze on the shoulder, and disappeared into a crowd of tourists.

Brill sighed heavily. He always felt morally diminished after spending time with Gramsci. The fact that this time it was he who needed the man's expertise, if it could be called that, left an aftertaste all the more sour. He moved closer to the Piaggio machine again and studied the papyrus lodged in its machinery. *What scroll was that?* How odd that he never noticed it before. There were hints of Greek letters, but he couldn't make out the words.

14

TORONTO

His meeting with Professor Pasternak left Marcus with a lot to absorb. Could Caesar have actually been planning to designate his illegitimate son with Cleopatra as his heir? He immediately went back to the library, looking for any clue that might support what her translation suggested: a potential alliance between two of the most famous political leaders in history.

Julius Caesar first encountered Cleopatra in Alexandria when she had herself smuggled into the Egyptian palace by way of a rolled-up carpet. Like a scroll, Marcus thought. In a flash, he imagined Kristi being unrolled from inside an exotic rug by Hellenistic court officials. A cheesy scenario, no better than a stripper popping out of a cake. He banished the thought from his mind.

The city of Alexandria had its fair share of scrolls; its monumental library boasted no less than seven hundred thousand papyrus books. It was bigger, more attractive, and more cosmopolitan than Rome.

The perfect location for a new East-meets-West empire, emulating the ambitions of its founder, Alexander the Great. Marcus knew the basics and could tap into his Europe 101 course lecture notes, still in his head, a grand sweeping survey course that was dubbed "From Plato to NATO." One of those classes described Alexander the Great's meteoric rise that ended with his sudden death in 323 BC. Warlords filled the political vacuum. Three superstates — Macedonia, the Seleucids in Asia, and Ptolemaic Egypt (Cleopatra's lineage) — had replaced him. All had been led by ambitious despots. The superstates rose at the expense of the old Greek city states, where citizens had once exercised political power (slaves and women excepted). All citizens were now reduced to inconsequence; the individual no longer played any role in the political process.

An idea took shape in Marcus's head — somewhat off-track, but that's what he liked about the study of history. Making links between disparate phenomena. The birth of Epicureanism and then Stoicism a few years later, both around 300 BC, took place in those harsh political conditions of rule by warlords. These new philosophies were therapeutic, promising psychological salvation. Epicureanism was a turning inward, the withdrawal from a society that had no use for its citizens beyond coughing up taxes and marching into battle. Stoicism's method for attaining peace of mind was emotional detachment. Both philosophies could be interpreted as a reaction to the new political landscape.

Marcus reflected sardonically that the current state of world affairs in which superstates diminished the power of citizens echoed what had happened twenty-three hundred years ago. But what were the new philosophies offering therapeutic salvation? Good question. But he was going off on a tangent. He read on.

After Caesar was assassinated, it was Piso and his daughter Calpurnia who obtained and made public the slain leader's legal papers, including the will that designated Octavian as his heir. And yet if the bombshell

Caesar scroll was authentic, Piso was ignoring Caesar's stated intentions by doing so.

Pasternak was probably correct: the staunch Roman in Piso would have recoiled at the idea of an Egyptian queen's child ruling the Republic. And as the father of Calpurnia, Piso would not have been keen to legitimize an out-of-wedlock child. Yet despite the propaganda levelled against her in Rome, Cleopatra may in fact have held Roman citizenship, either through her ancestry or as a gift of Caesar. Then there was the fact that Piso loved the Hellenistic culture which Cleopatra embodied.

After the murder of Caesar, Piso was sent by the Senate on a dangerous diplomatic mission to the camp of Mark Antony. No word survives about what transpired before the man suddenly disappeared from recorded history, leaving behind his splendiferous Villa dei Papiri.

As for Caesarion, the young boy who'd been shuttled back to Alexandria in his mother's arms became little more than a footnote in history books. When the final civil war ended with Octavian's overwhelming victory and the suicides of Cleopatra and Mark Antony, Caesarion was fleeing Egypt with his tutor, following a plan crafted by his desperate mother. Perhaps to India or to some remote eastern kingdom where he might live out his days protected as a prince. But his tutor betrayed Caesarion, and the seventeen-year-old boy was swiftly hunted down and killed by Octavian's soldiers.

Marcus was thoroughly enjoying his plunge back into historical research. He'd never finished his Ph.D., bailing because he lacked scholarly stick-to-it-iveness at the time. But now he was getting another crack at scholarship. The Caesar scroll belonged to Marcus, if it belonged to anyone. It could be the springboard of a reinvigorated career.

But at what cost to his personal safety? He recalled his ransacked hotel room in Naples. Had someone been out to get him? Or his scroll? A knot deep within his core, a knot that had formed when Ballard was killed and the scroll disappeared, tightened and loosened and tightened again. That old panic attack about losing his life. Tame it. Tamp it down, tamp it down like tobacco in one of his uncle's pipes. That would have been Gerald's advice.

15

UNIVERSITY OF WATERLOO

Margaret Pasternak was working on a translation of Cicero's *The Nature of the Gods*, which more than two thousand years ago had helped make Greek philosophy accessible to a Latin-speaking audience. She wanted to do something similar for contemporary readers by taking Cicero's lovely Latin and rendering it into English. She hoped it might be the sort of publication that could burst the confines of academia. The jacket might declare: *Two millennia ago, thinkers with fewer technological distractions could focus more clearly on the fundamentals of human happiness . . .*

Her office phone rang and when she picked up, Pasternak was surprised to hear the unmistakable, reedy voice of her academic mentor. David Brill almost never called her. But she had contacted him recently when she needed a second opinion on a passage in that curious text crafted, quite impressively, to be a letter from Caesar.

She had all but worshipped Brill when he was her thesis advisor at Oxford. He had his quirks but possessed far fewer eccentricities than most classics professors she knew. Yes, he once leapt on a desk to strike a pose while reading Sophocles and was known to mutter "Go to hell" in ancient Greek when sufficiently annoyed. He would drop the name of Bucephalus, Alexander the Great's horse, in casual conversation. But Brill was above all a laser-focused scholar and considered a top-flight papyrologist working on the Herculaneum scrolls.

"I'm sorry to bother you like this, Maggie."

"Oh, it's never a bother to hear from you, professor. How are you?"

"Fine, fine. I just wanted to follow up on something we spoke about. That little freelance job you were working on? The imaginative letter regarding Caesar? What was that for exactly?"

"I don't really know, to tell you the truth. It was written by an antiquities dealer who had some background in classics. The dealer's nephew was the one who commissioned my translation. A very rough translation. The nephew was short on details. Why?"

"I am now wondering if it might have been taken from an actual papyrus."

"No way! An actual letter of Caesar's?"

"Well, I'm by no means certain. I'm just looking into this."

"That would be incredible! But, well, the people who brought it to me didn't strike me as black-market types. Or I'd be very surprised. The nephew's friend is a respected newspaper journalist. But I have to say, the text was remarkably convincing. It even had archaic spelling and lots of lacunae."

"So it struck you as authentic? Or possibly so?"

"I saw no obvious errors. I did wonder about a possible forgery scam and even raised the question. The nephew strenuously denied such a thing. And there was one curious aspect. The letter ended prematurely. I asked to see the rest of the text but was told there wasn't any more to see."

"That doesn't rule out its authenticity," Brill said. "Did you ask where the rest of the text might be?"

"Well, the nephew wasn't very forthcoming, and I didn't press him on the issue. I've been juggling a lot lately and scrambled to get this done for some pocket money. Which I can use. My head has been completely buried in Cicero these days."

Silence from his end made her realize that he didn't recall the Cicero translation that had been consuming her, though she'd mentioned it to him more than once. "My Cicero project?" she reminded him.

"Oh, right," he said, sounding distracted.

She gave up and returned to his question. "About that Caesar letter. What papyrus could have included it?"

"Please keep this under your hat, Maggie. But there are rumours here in Naples of a 'Caesar scroll' on the black market."

She gasped. "From the Villa?"

"So it would seem."

"That's unbelievable."

"Indeed. So, do you happen to have a copy of the text you might send me? And the name of the individual you did the work for?"

MARCUS SINCLAIR SEEMED AN UNLIKELY PERSON to have a papyrus in his possession. Brill had met him briefly at the conference in Herculaneum, a scraggly-haired junior college teacher with no expertise in the field. He and the poor fellow who died, Ballard, were always together, sharing private jokes, quizzing those in the know. Newcomers to the conference, taking a sort of mischievous glee in their outsider status. On the other hand, Ballard appeared to know his stuff when it came to imaging technology; he'd been serious about harnessing the latest digital technology for the scrolls. Brill had to admit that even he was encouraged, dazzled even, by the prospect of Google lending a hand.

But where would Marcus Sinclair's uncle have acquired such a treasure? And how had the scroll been unrolled? Had it still been rolled up or unrolled when Sinclair got it? Pasternak had no answers to these questions.

Perhaps it was an attempted forgery. That would not be surprising for an antiquities dealer with scholarly pretensions. If so, according to Pasternak, the forgery was the work of an expert. Was the uncle tied to criminal elements in the antiquities market? Wherever the text came from, whatever it was, it was now circulating. Gramsci clearly knew about it, and Gramsci was his link to the criminal world. He had no desire to get mixed up in less-than-legal schemes. But he couldn't help but wonder whether these rumours about a Caesar scroll could be connected to the theft of his own knapsack and all his hard-earned research notes.

Brill was tempted to turn a blind eye to all of this. Life threw up enough difficulties without him actively seeking new ones. Nose to the grindstone, that was his philosophy.

But if the Caesar scroll were authentic? The repercussions would be astounding, suggesting that there might have been an entirely different course for Western civilization. Caesarion, not Octavian, the heir to Julius Caesar? No Emperor Augustus and his single-handed creation of the Roman Empire? Instead a true son of Caesar and Cleopatra based in Rome *and* Alexandria?

Brill considered two avenues. Try to pry more information from the unsavoury but well-informed Gramsci. Or meet up with Marcus Sinclair and try to draw him out.

16

HAZELTON ROW

Kristi emerged from the Bay Street subway station into the posh shopping mecca that was Yorkville. Not her cup of matcha. But she had to admit they'd nicely upgraded the area with attractive lanes and novel public spaces, like that enormous slab of rock where you could climb and sit and watch the glitzy world go by. Chanel and Versace she could live without, but she might pop into Whole Foods later.

She rounded the corner at Hazelton, eyed the parked luxury vehicles, the high-end art galleries, and the signage displayed on well-manicured heritage buildings. Alpha, Signal, Global Fixed Income Experts, not to mention Injekt Aesthetics Bar and Elite Body Sculpture. This was a far cry from Starving Artist Waffles in her part of town.

Gerald's condo, at least from the outside, was not as glamorous as she expected. A four-storey, prosaic building of red brick with French-style balconies its sole embellishment. It was likelier more impressive inside; she knew that his condo occupied the entire top floor. Kristi lifted a lever that opened the wrought-iron gate. Decorative stone vases were set on pedestals amid an unruly array of trees and hedges. A jungle, she thought, though not a Jungle Bar. Trevor Ballard was uppermost on her mind these days. At the main entrance, she pressed the button on the intercom for Sinclair.

"JULIUS CAESAR. GOOD GUY OR BAD GUY?"

Marcus had carried a pot of tea into the elegant salon, which was filled with vases, mosaics, and marble columns. It would have to be their last meeting for a while, since he was heading off to a symposium about the Herculaneum scrolls in Los Angeles. And Kristi herself would soon be leaving for Naples to research her investigative piece on Ballard's murder.

"I'll go with bad," Kristi answered. "Military leaders are bad more often than they're good."

"Well, your instincts are right in that a great number of Gauls were killed or enslaved by his soldiers." Marcus poured their tea from a pot decorated with Hellenic motifs.

"So," Kristi said, "he was a mass murderer?"

"You could put it that way."

"I'm only interested in history," she said, "insofar as it's influenced the present. The rest are all names of great men and great battles and great long stretches of boredom."

"Fair enough. But given what we're facing with the scroll, you might want to bone up on the great Caesar."

"Give me the elevator pitch. A hundred words or less."

"Okay. Let's see. Caesar's name became a synonym for 'dictator' in several languages: *kaiser* and *czar*, for example. But Caesar himself was more than just a strongman who concentrated all power in his own hands. He tried to fix a system of government, the Late Roman Republic, that was taking over the known world but had become dysfunctional. He was a populist but progressive. And at the same time an intellectual and a great writer."

"You forgot the mass murderer part."

"Right. Anyway, debate still rages about whether Rome would have done better with or without him. Civil war followed his murder. Famous victims included Cicero, Cleopatra, Brutus, Mark Antony. No shortage of dramatic material. Finally Octavian, as Pasternak reminded us, Caesar's great-nephew, emerged victorious, changed his name to Augustus, and Rome went from being a republic to an empire."

"And the rest is history," she said.

"Touché."

"Interesting. No, really, it is. And I'd like to learn more someday. But we have some pressing issues in the here and now."

"Sure." Marcus sipped his tea, not used to having his history lessons cut short. Some network of neural synapses inside him actually missed the classroom.

Kristi scanned the eye candy in the room, focusing on a small, multi-coloured Roman statue.

"So," she said, "there's a scroll somewhere that would have changed history, or the writing of history, in a big way and turned two thousand years of scholarship on its head, right?"

"Correct."

"And it's a thing of value. Maybe lots of value."

"Material value. But how much? I haven't the foggiest. In the nineteenth century, Britain sent eighteen kangaroos to Naples for the same number of scrolls. So, factoring out inflation, each scroll is worth approximately one kangaroo."

"Seriously?"

"The kangaroo story actually happened. But yes, you're right — a letter from Caesar designating his son with Cleopatra as heir would be worth a king's ransom. Just imagine the bidding war among foundations, private collectors, universities, European institutions."

"Okay," she said. "Let's think this through. Ballard was in Naples to research and make contacts for the technological means of deciphering the Herculaneum scrolls, which are too carbonized, too beat up, to be unrolled physically."

"Except for those scrolls that already have been unrolled."

"Yes, but nobody cares about those scrolls. Old news. What people are really hoping for is some eureka tech solution. Ballard being one of those people. He's there in Naples, educating himself, networking, and suddenly, lo and behold, a new scroll — *your* scroll — falls into his lap."

"That's a coup for him," Marcus said, "because all the other scrolls, whatever shape they're in, are under lock and key in the Officina, unavailable to non-scholars. So Ballard has something to work with. He lets it be known to his contacts."

Kristi said, "It all makes sense so far. But who would want to kill him? And why?"

"To use an expression Cicero liked, *cui bono*? Who benefits?"

From outside came the wail of a car alarm.

"Or the opposite," Kristi said. "Who's threatened?"

"The Officina? With its territorial mentality? But a new technology for unrolling the scrolls would solve a lot of their challenges. And give them international exposure. It doesn't add up.

"Obviously someone wanted my scroll. Keep in mind Ballard also had my photocopy of the text Laszlo had already unrolled. The text of the Caesar letter. Whoever killed Ballard must have known that."

Kristi fished her cell out of her bag. "When I'm in Naples, I'll look up Cipressi, you know, the physicist who met with Ballard? He may know more than he told me over the phone. Hold on," she punched in her password, "I'm going to email him right now. And just to remind you: do not reveal my source to anyone. He spoke to me off the record."

Marcus held his cup in both hands, warming them while she

keyed the email. He wished he was going to Naples with her. But the Herculaneum symposium in Los Angeles was not something he could miss. In particular, a lecture on tracking down old papyri was on the agenda. It was currently his best bet for getting some clues to the whereabouts of Gerald's scroll.

"Done," Kristi said. "Let's see if he even responds. What else? Oh, I located the archaeologist you mentioned, the guy who ranted against Google and Ballard. It wasn't hard, given the archaeology tattoos you described. His name is Spiros Dima. Sounds very reasonable on the phone. Says he was in the National Library on the day Ballard was killed, claims he never saw him, that he was in the big reading room checking some eighteenth-century archaeological records. He even emailed me a receipt of books loaned to him that day."

"Okay. I guess that holds up. But doth he protest too much with the receipts? Borrowing books and murdering someone are not mutually exclusive."

"Hey, I never asked you. Where were you when you first heard Ballard was dead?"

"I was across the street from our hotel. At a small convenience store, buying some bottled water. I remember hearing the ambulance arrive. A few hours later, I bumped into Auger, who told me."

"Who's that?"

"Olivier Auger; you know, the French papyrologist."

"Right. Auger. Could *he* be a suspect?"

"No way. He's the bon vivant Parisian academic I told you about. Not a care in the world aside from papyrological puzzles. He seemed to be amused by everything and anything."

"That means nothing. I'm putting an asterisk next to his name."

Kristi placed her phone on a side table with classical Greek adornment, authentic or not, and glanced around a living room filled with artwork and collectibles.

"This place *is* pretty amazing."

"Gerald called it his 'den of antiquity.'"

"Nice."

She sipped some green tea.

"But I'm not sure about that painted statue," she said. "It looks a bit over the top."

It was a familiar statue of Augustus, painted with colour, giving Rome's first emperor brown hair, a blue tunic, a crimson toga.

"It's a colour reconstruction," Marcus said. "By Laszlo, actually. Gerald had him paint it. There's a school of thought that says all these pure white statues are misleading, that Greek and Roman statues were originally painted but that the colours had faded by the time European collectors got their hands on them. Only later did pure whiteness become the ideal classical aesthetic. Gerald was an early believer in the colourful version of antiquity. He was ahead of his time."

She drained her cup of tea.

"You were fond of him."

"Still am. Maybe even more now, six months since he's been gone. I think of him way more often these days than I did when he was alive. Living here. Can you smell the apple-flavoured pipe tobacco he smoked? There are bags and bags of it all over the place, so I can keep breathing in memories far into the future. I'm constantly stumbling onto things like his Rolodex and address books filled with the names of dealers, galleries, fixers. I feel bad that I never was interested in all this stuff when he was alive."

"It's natural. It wasn't your area of specialization."

"*I* wasn't his area of specialization either. But he found time for me. After my father disappeared and my mother had to get a job, I was afraid to go to some first day of school. It was probably kindergarten, actually. So he took me. He walked into the building with me, right up to the classroom door, and said he'd be right there until I was okay.

I saw him in the doorway, dressed in his dapper three-piece suit as usual, while I sat down on the floor with the other kids. And just seeing him there made everything all right."

He poured her more tea from a rust-coloured pot, the one with Hellenic motifs, another antiquity maybe, or a copy, and she touched his forearm, stopping him from pouring.

"What?"

For a few seconds, she froze, a radiant statue. "That's enough tea for me, thanks."

He'd contemplated a kiss. But the moment came and went.

"I have some names from Gerald's Rolodex. A few seem to be tech contacts, all out of town, a bunch in Italy. I'm going to start calling them. Good timing for that conference in L.A. All the propeller-heads working on the papyri will be there. A who's who of Herculaneum."

"And how will that help your cause?"

"I have a plan. I'm going to quietly put the word out that I've inherited some money from my uncle and am looking to purchase a scroll from Herculaneum."

"Well, be careful. Who knows what's going on behind the scenes of that world?"

"I hear you. But I figure it's a lot safer than going back to Naples."

"Maybe for you," she said, gleefully clapping out a drumroll on her knees. "But I can't wait to get to Italy."

17

CENTRO STORICO

Zuccarello relished the pleasurable chaos of driving her Vespa in the core of the city. A game of chicken. Survival of the fastest. Waiting for a red light to change, she could hear multiple text messages chiming on her phone. Always something with this job! She prevented a motorcycle from cutting her off by refusing to blink first and soon eased her scooter into a parking spot. She stopped for an espresso on Via Toledo, savouring a moment of freedom from the work headaches that inevitably awaited her.

Giuseppe, looking perturbed, was standing outside her office. No more clinging. *Basta.* He's a grown man. She didn't want to report this, try to have him transferred and get tangled up in a bureaucratic complaint that would only interfere with her career path.

He said, "The toxicology and blood work report for Trevor Ballard came in."

"And?"

"Evidence that some sort of synthetic opioid was in his body."

"What?" She felt the sort of jolt normally caused by a double espresso. "What do they think happened? An overdose?"

"It's not clear yet. They have to examine his clothes and stuff for traces of the drug."

"Also, what about those nitrile gloves?" Zuccarello asked. "Why were there *two* pairs of them?"

"It's possible there were two assailants. Each of them wearing the gloves."

"That's a lot of assailants in a small hotel room," she said. "Also, there was that man with the hat and sunglasses recorded on the hotel surveillance camera. One man, not two."

Zuccarello considered the fact pattern. The National Science Police report categorized that blood as "expiatory spatter" — blood emanating from an internal injury and mixed with air expelled from the mouth via coughing. Might it have been an opioid addiction that went one lethal step too far? No, the victim's computer and phone were missing, which all but ruled out suicide or overdose. Plus those nitrile gloves.

She regarded Giuseppe for a long moment, resisting an urge to hug her ex-lover, then walked by him, plunked her helmet and bag on the floor, and took the seat behind her desk. She fixed her gaze on the brick wall outside her window.

"Where does an American tourist find opioids here?" she said.

"It's not difficult," Giuseppe said, "believe me. It's Napoli we're talking about. Besides, he probably had the drugs with him when he arrived here."

"A few weeks' worth? He'd been here a while. And if it was his personal supply from the U.S. for pain or addiction, he probably wouldn't have overdosed as easily as when using something new."

Giuseppe spread out his open palms in a gesture of "who knows?"

"And the Jungle Bar."

"What about it?"

"The other clue in Ballard's room. The business card. Maybe he got the opioid at the club. You didn't learn anything there?"

"No. Nobody there recognized his photo."

"We have to retrace Ballard's footsteps from the time he set foot in Napoli. Who did he meet? Go over all your notes again. And go back to the Jungle Bar. Maybe you'll get lucky."

Giuseppe flashed his sly smile. "Lucky? At the Jungle Bar?"

"You know what I mean."

18

PACIFIC PALISADES

Marcus was admiring the life-sized statues known as the Herculaneum Dancers. The originals were pulled out of the ground from the Villa dei Papiri in 1754. These were replicas.

The entire villa was a replica.

Located in the hills above Los Angeles, the Getty Villa was a remarkably faithful copy of the Villa dei Papiri. It was the brainchild of oil magnate J. Paul Getty, richest man in the world, semi-recluse, avid collector of antiquities. The actual Villa dei Papiri lay six thousand miles away in Herculaneum, buried beneath seventy feet of hardened volcanic mud. But Getty's architect was able to base his design on a ground plan of the Villa made in the eighteenth century. When the Getty opened in 1974, architecture critics turned up their noses, but the public instantly loved the place.

Marcus was at the Getty for a one-day symposium on the Herculaneum scrolls. The top players in the business of deciphering papyri were attending, including Professor David Brill. Brill had emailed Marcus, asking if they could have a chat at the event. Marcus was apprehensive: What did Brill want to know? But it couldn't hurt to talk to him. After all, Marcus was planning to discreetly buttonhole experts there about where a papyrus scroll from Herculaneum might be purchased.

"My talk will be boilerplate," Brill was now saying, "on how the latest technology is assisting my translation of the Philodemus book, *On Friendship*, Book Two. It's still a work in progress, slower progress than planned, I'm afraid, given the theft of my knapsack and the working facsimile that was inside."

He looked at Marcus intently, his clever eyes measuring him from beneath the brim of his straw hat. Marcus already knew about the backpack theft from an email from the Friends of Herculaneum. "I'm sorry about that," he said. "I read about it in the newsletter."

Could Brill actually think, Marcus wondered, that he had something to do with the stolen knapsack? Was that why he wanted to meet?

They were in the rectangular garden, facing one of the "Herculaneum Dancers." Not so long ago, Marcus had admired the five originals, life-size bronzes of barefoot Greek women, in the Naples archaeology museum. Here were their doppelgängers arrayed around the Villa's pool.

"These statues are pale imitations of the original bronze ones," Brill said.

Marcus agreed. One particular statue that he remembered very well exerted an erotic tug on him. She was fastening or unfastening — he preferred to think the latter — a shoulder brooch that held together her short-sleeved garment. Her corkscrew curls were coiffed to elegant perfection. A hint of revulsion lay on her full lips. Unlike the other austere statues in the group with their expressionless gazes, her eyes, inlaid with ivory, communicated something ill at ease, as if aware she must disrobe for gawking strangers in the distant future. She had more reason than the other statues to worry. Marcus had read that in 1944, the statue was taken from safekeeping at an Italian abbey by a Luftwaffe division. She ended up in Berlin as a birthday gift for Hermann Goering.

"And this pool," Brill continued, "is not as deep as the original. It's only eighteen inches to the bottom because the parking garage is right below. If it were any deeper, the city of L.A. would insist on a lifeguard. So it's not perfectly authentic. But then, what is? Even the original 'Dancers,' in Herculaneum were probably copies of Greek statues. And focus on the original findspots in the Villa ignores the likelihood that the force of the volcanic eruption may have thrown the objects helter-skelter from one room to the next or from one level to the one below. So I'm not much of a purist when it comes to the archaeology of the site."

Brill paused.

"But I *am* about the papyri."

He again levelled that steely gaze at Marcus. "Which brings me to the subject I wanted to speak to you about. I'm fairly well connected in this business; that's what thirty-nine years of work in one small corner of the academic world does for you. And it's come to my attention that there may be a scroll that has slipped through official fingers. A scroll, dare I say, of great interest."

Marcus took a moment to register what Brill said. How would he know that Marcus had inherited a scroll? Of the handful of people aware of Gerald's scroll, two were dead — Ballard and Gerald himself.

They were standing by the pool, facing another bronze statue. The "Drunken Satyr" was half man, half goat, collapsed on a lion skin, one arm lifted free, a finger signalling, as if to say, *One more jug of wine, slave!* His lips in a toothless grimace above a goatee, his thick hair dishevelled.

"If you don't mind me asking," Marcus said, "how did you learn about all this?"

"It's a small world, the world of papyrology. There are few secrets. I'm not at liberty to reveal my sources, but two people from different areas of the business have told me about it."

"Two people?"

"I won't start naming names. Just the same way as I will not repeat anything you might tell me in confidence. I'm surprised, frankly, that a scroll connected to Julius Caesar has escaped my notice for as long as it has."

It occurred to Marcus that Pasternak also knew about his scroll or suspected as much. Plus he'd told the police in Naples after Ballard was killed, though the detective seemed profoundly uninterested. Marcus felt that knot in his gut tightening again. "I'm not sure I can help you that much," he said. "I mean, I don't have the actual scroll."

"But you have the text?"

"I have the first part of the text. I inherited the scroll from my uncle, who got someone to try unrolling it on a homemade Piaggio machine. After one segment was unrolled, they couldn't get any farther. The papyrus layers were too fused together."

"Remarkable. May I ask where all of this transpired?" Brill seemed to pronounce the word *remarkable* in italics. As if he didn't quite buy Marcus's explanation.

"It was partially unrolled in Toronto. I then brought the remainder of the scroll with me to Naples, except for that small segment that my uncle managed to unroll."

"And the present whereabouts of this scroll?" Brill asked.

"Stolen, presumably. I lent it to Trevor Ballard. It disappeared when he was killed."

"Oh, my!" Brill said. He seemed uncharacteristically at a loss for words.

They had walked the length of the reflecting pool, which was framed by lush, symmetrical landscaping. At the far end, they turned into the colonnaded porch and headed back to the Villa, passing a long row of Doric columns and frescoes.

"These illusionistic frescoes on the porticoes don't actually exist at the real villa," Brill said. "They are an incongruous embellishment, illusions in more than one way. And you've got me wondering about this Julius Caesar scroll. If it has indeed gone missing, we can't be sure of its authenticity. It might also be an illusion. That is to say, a fake."

"I don't think so," Marcus said. "The whole story sounds very believable to me."

"There's no way to verify that without the actual papyrus," Brill said.

"Any ideas you have for me would be much appreciated. I'd like to figure out how to find it. Plus, I have some funds which I inherited, money that I could use to, um, perhaps purchase any scroll that might come to market?"

Brill thought with less distaste than usual of the man named Gramsci. He also felt duty bound to notify the police in Naples. But he was not thinking of how to help this Sinclair fellow with a dubious connection to a potentially bombshell papyrus.

"It's a puzzle," he said. "Like all the papyri. I doubt I can do much for you."

19

CAFFÈ GAMBRINUS

After checking into her Airbnb, Kristi packed some essentials into a knapsack, opened Google Maps on her phone, and set out for the first destination on her list. Her investigative piece on Trevor Ballard could hardly be complete without a trip to Naples. The story could use some colour, not to mention some notion as to why and how Ballard died. With a little luck, being in the field would fill in some blanks.

And for her own personal reasons, she was delighted to be in Italy. For so many years, she was juggling a demanding job with being a single mom; jetting off to Europe was something that other people did. Raising Alexander alone hadn't been easy, and it limited romantic relationships. Kristi sized up prospective partners based on the influence they'd have on her son. It was challenging enough to find a combination friend/lover/yogi. Add father figure to the mix, and the odds got exponential. But her sacrifice had been worth it.

Alexander had turned out remarkably solid — smart, low-maintenance, a young adult whose company she genuinely enjoyed. Now he was off in Vancouver, a college graduate in math and computer science, working at a startup.

Kristi walked west along the Spaccanapoli, a street lined with gelaterias and pizzerias, pulsating with tourists and motorbikes. At Piazza Bellini, she stopped to get her bearings and then continued to Via Toledo, merging with the sort of exuberant crowd that pours out of a sports stadium. She noticed many shirts with banal slogans like *Stay Real* and *Take Your Time*. The same lack of imagination applied to many shop names so lame that she gleefully jotted them down in her notepad: Cool Type, Vanity, Easy Chic. So much for the art of good writing. She continued down the elegant commercial boulevard, passing the big beige Banco di Napoli, where the pedestrianized stretch began and fresh air blew in from the sea. Naples, she reminded herself, was a Mediterranean city.

In the distance, she saw gold leaf letters *MB* on a handsome pink-and-grey building. As she got closer, more letters came into focus: *GAMB*. Then: *GAMBRINUS*. This was her first destination. Marcus had sung the praises of the café for its coffee, pastries, and setting.

At a nearby traffic roundabout crowned with a gushing fountain, engines revved and horns blared. She crossed the street and stepped inside the café, which was decorated with grand mirrors and gilded chandeliers. A barista in a chocolate-brown jacket, crisp white shirt, and bow tie shifted the gears of a gleaming espresso machine as if it were his Ferrari.

She read some of the old newspaper clips adorning one wall. Oldest café in the city. Shut down in the 1930s for being anti-fascist. Numerous illustrious patrons.

Way back in 1860, the Gambrinus invented the *caffè sospeso* — a suspended coffee, meaning buyers could purchase a coffee that would go toward a future customer who could not afford the beverage.

Charmed by the concept, she made the purchase and placed the receipt as instructed in a large moka jar. Someone needy would pluck her receipt out of the jar and buy a coffee with perfect dignity. Outside, she located one of the few unoccupied small tables.

Cappuccino cups and saucers proclaimed *Gambrinus Napoli* in flowery script. The café's coat of arms — a bearded man raising a glass while sitting on a keg of wine — was stamped on napkins and engraved on glasses.

Kristi ordered a cappuccino from a waiter wearing a black bow tie and cream vest, his lapel embroidered in golden letters. At five and a half euros, it was an exorbitant coffee, but the tab included a stellar view of the gorgeous piazza, opera house, domed shopping mall, Pantheon-style church, and the sprawling pink-and-grey Royal Palace. Sipping her cappuccino, she gazed across the piazza. The Officina was located in a remote section of the National Library, which in turn was located in the Royal Palace. She prepared to do what she'd been doing her entire journalistic career, whether it was tearing open a UN food shipment for a starving Congolese crowd or showing desperate earthquake refugees in Haiti how to sneak around security into an embassy compound. Kristi was going to take matters into her own hands.

20

PACIFIC PALISADES

The Getty Villa was nestled in a lush hillside of olive trees, sycamores, and pines overlooking the Pacific Ocean. But Marcus's mind was elsewhere, trying to figure out how he might locate his scroll. To that end, he made every effort to speak with papyrus experts during breaks in the symposium.

The first lecture, on the topic of Mount Vesuvius, was delivered in the Getty auditorium by an eminent volcanologist, John Sommerville, a tall man in his fifties with a mushroom cloud of white hair. He was wearing a navy blazer, baggy cargo pants, and hiking boots, the lower, geological part of his wardrobe presumably being his usual dress code and the blazer a concession to the lecture circuit. After he bound up to the dais, only the blazer showed.

Sommerville wasted no time with pleasantries and got straight to the point: "Mount Vesuvius is guaranteed to erupt again. The question is not if, but when."

He noted that in the modern period of Vesuvius — the past twenty thousand years — there had been four major eruptions. The most recent had been the infamous eruption of AD 79. Aside from those major eruptions, he said, there had been a number of smaller ones. These were still powerful enough, at least in one case, to blow the top of the mountain off. Another left eighteen thousand people dead.

Sommerville said that between 1631 and 1944, the volcano was in near-continuous activity. "That meant an eruption every ten or twenty or thirty years. That's about three hundred years during which the volcano was active. Then, after the 1944 eruption, the volcano shut down. It has been ominously quiet ever since. A period of quiet which concerns scientists in terms of what we might expect for the next eruption."

On the wall behind the speaker appeared a high-resolution aerial photo of the volcano showing trails snaking up to the crater.

MARCUS THOUGHT BACK TO HIS OWN HIKE UP VESUVIUS. It was the third day of the Herculaneum conference, and the agenda featured not a serious hike but instead the easy, touristy way to ascend the mountain. Conference attendees were bused to a staging area some two hundred fifty metres below the summit. The early morning souvenir stands were already doing a brisk trade in lava necklaces and erotic Pompeii calendars.

From there, it was a steep walk up a dusty path lined with wooden guard rails. The dreary, overcast weather meant few photo-worthy views. Marcus darted ahead with Olivier Auger while Ballard and two younger papyrologists, Christoph and Lorenzo, lagged behind. The rest of the delegates were even farther back.

"It is bizarre to be here," Auger said. "Despite what anyone says, the experts, the monitoring . . . this mountain could explode at any minute."

"And if it does," Marcus said, "as an Epicurean, death is nothing to you, right?"

"*Exactement.*"

A nearby yellow sign warned, *Caution: Falling Rocks.*

Marcus said, "I'm not sure I find that so reassuring. I mean, we're still talking about the annihilation of consciousness."

"Are you troubled by where your consciousness was before you were alive?" asked Auger.

"That seems different. A false equivalent."

Auger stumbled on some stones and Marcus caught his arm, steadying him.

"I'm not trying to convert anyone," Auger said with a Gallic shrug. "The Epicurean system is not for *tout le monde.* It was not for all the Greeks two thousand years ago. And I'm in accord that the subject of death is a difficult one. Maybe the objective is to not think about mortality very much. The Greeks did not think about living after dying. Not much, in Homer or in other places. They thought that man could not talk about the divinity."

"What about all those Greek myths?"

"Ah. The big, beautiful facade! Yes. The sacred was not something we could comprehend. Or . . ." Auger paused to chug some water. "The only way the Greeks could connect with the sacred was with sacrifice. Bizarre to us. But it was their *façon* of communicating with the gods."

Marcus picked up a pebble honeycombed with bubbles and wondered whether it was a piece of lava or pumice, some chunk of evidence from the infamous eruption.

Auger continued, "But you know, the Epicureans were very *fidèle* to the rituals of religion."

"So you don't think they were closet atheists? Just pretending in order to get along in a world full of believers?"

"No, I think they really believed in the gods. Did you know that several Epicureans were religious officials in ancient Rome?"

"That seems odd to me. I mean, wasn't the point of ritual, of believing in the gods, that they would do something for you? And the Epicureans didn't believe the gods could, or would bother, doing anything for us."

"That is an interesting point. When life was good, it was evidence that ritual sacrifices were working and obviously the gods existed. And when life was bad, when bad things happened — natural disasters — insufficient ritual was blamed. For that reason, our friend Philodemus was forced to leave a town in Sicily after a plague."

"Because he was an unbeliever?"

"Epicureans had a bad reputation for this," Auger said. "Unjustified, in my own opinion. But certainly their argument that the gods existed but were laissez-faire was a problem."

They'd made it to the vast crater, thirteen hundred metres above sea level, and were leaning on its rim, surveying the Martian terrain and peering into a volcanic abyss.

"This is a lot like looking into a big microscope but seeing nothing," Auger said.

"And what," Marcus asked, "are you trying to decipher down there?"

Before he could answer, they heard Ballard approaching, along with Lorenzo and Christoph. "Voila!" Auger said. "Here comes our hero from Google to solve all our problems. Just put faith in technology, n'est-ce pas?"

The trio, deep in animated conversation, joined them.

"So this is where it all comes from!" Ballard draped his arms over the wood railing and leaned over the rim of Vesuvius. "I mean, all the scrolls; you have them thanks to this natural wonder."

"What took you guys so long?"

"We were solving the problem of unrolling the papyri," Lorenzo said.

"Undoing the damage that this volcano did," Ballard said. He took a swig from a water bottle inscribed with *Silicon H2O*.

"That is true," Christoph said. "But if it wasn't for this volcano, the papyrus scrolls would never have survived."

Auger turned away from the crater and pointed outwards to the sea.

"Normally there is a fantastic view of Capri. Pity it's so cloudy today."

Ballard checked his cell phone; there was no coverage. He tossed a stone into the crater.

"I would not want to die from this eruption," Christoph said. "The pyroclastic flow gives you no chance to escape. It boils your brains inside your skull."

"Lovely," Marcus said.

Auger said, "You remember what Caesar said about dying? When he was asked during a banquet what is the best way for a man to die, he said, 'It is a quick death with no warning.' And the next day, he himself was dead."

AUGER'S WORDS THAT DAY NOW SEEMED ODD TO MARCUS. What was it that Kristi had said about him? That she'd put an asterisk next to his name?

In the Getty auditorium, while the lecturer droned on about Vesuvius, the death of Ballard felt abstract. Like a statistic that had long ago been inserted into his head. Yet a statistic he was determined to make sense of. How much of the lecture had he zoned out for? Marcus rubbed his tired eyes and forced his attention back to the speaker.

Sommerville was characterizing the two types of volcanic eruptions. "They can be effusive or explosive. Effusive means it produces lava. Explosive means a pyroclastic flow: a lethal outpouring of gas, ash, and particles." Lava hadn't been involved in the eruption of AD 79, he explained. That eruption was explosive, which had two results: pumice falling from the sky and pyroclastic flows. Forced to choose between the two, you'd want pumice.

"If pumice was falling on your head, it would hurt, but you wouldn't be burning. Pumice is not very heavy; it's like shaving cream that has hardened. If you were to step on it, you'd crush it. But if you're caught up in a pyroclastic flow — look out! Prepare to meet your maker! We're talking about a nasty cloud of gas and particles. Rock and ash weaponized by gas that's five hundred degrees Celsius moving at a rate of one hundred kilometres an hour. You can't outrun it. It's as fast as an avalanche moving down a slope."

After describing in detail how the eruption buried Pompeii and Herculaneum, Sommerville glanced at his watch and said he was happy to field a few questions.

A baritone voice from the back of the audience asked, "When is the next big eruption most likely to happen?"

Sommerville removed his chunky watch and placed it on the lectern. "It might occur in a few thousand years. Or it might occur tomorrow."

Which told Marcus there was no time to waste in pursuing his investigation. But still, he might learn something at this conference which could point him in the right direction. The next lectures, to be delivered consecutively, were titled "Recreating the Villa of the Papyri in Malibu"; "Scribes and Scholars on the Bay of Naples"; and "Scroll Survivor: The Search for Papyri." Marcus was most interested in the last one, to be given by Professor Roger Smith of Brigham Young University. Marcus knew that BYU, a Mormon college in Provo, Utah, had a vested interest in the papyri, which was to find more documentation from the time of Jesus. However, despite the religious agenda, its scientific credentials in the field were impeccable, and it had helped a lot in the reading of the papyri.

During the symposium's coffee breaks, Marcus circulated, recognizing several faces from the Herculaneum conference. When the moment seemed right, he'd mention that he'd come into an inheritance and was looking to purchase a papyrus. His story produced skeptical looks, and he feared he was coming off as an amateur with an unhealthy obsession. Which he was starting to feel might in fact be the case. At the conference in Herculaneum, being with Trevor Ballard of Google conferred a certain legitimacy on him. Now he was on his own and felt very much like the outsider he was.

He spotted Kurt Jensen, a Michigan-based academic and one of the speakers. Jensen had been aloof and standoffish at the Italian conference; Marcus never felt comfortable in his presence. The shaggy-haired scholar originally from California had been glued to his phone while other scholars gossiped wildly about him in hushed tones: he'd bought a winery in Chile; he was moving to Singapore; his wife, an accomplished pianist, was the real brains in the household; he was somehow connected to the antiquities market.

Jensen recognized Marcus and was more receptive than he'd been in Italy. "Terrible about Ballard," he said. He spoke with a slight stutter. "The talk about Vesuvius put him in my head. That was where I met him. We walked up the volcano together a little bit and then got separated."

"Same here," Marcus said. He then told Jensen that he had come into some money and was in the market for a papyrus scroll, ideally one from Herculaneum.

Jensen's hand shook, and he nearly spilled his coffee onto his jacket. "Look," Jensen mumbled. "I don't have much time. My lecture on scribes and scholars is up next. In, um," he checked his phone, "thirteen minutes."

Marcus asked if he knew anyone who might help him purchase a papyrus.

"Not really," Jensen said softly. He glanced around before replying that he had one possible lead. Attending the symposium was someone named Connor Peets, who worked for the Holy Books Foundation. "He's in the business of procuring scrolls," Jensen said. "Perhaps he'll have an idea."

One more lecture and then a break for lunch. Marcus was eyeing the name badges, looking in vain for Connor Peets. The lectures themselves were tedious and offered no new leads for finding his scroll. It wasn't until the end of the day, during the closing cocktail hour, that Marcus spotted the name tag belonging to Peets. A short, balding man dressed in a navy blazer, red tie, and grey slacks, he was on his way out of the Getty. Marcus waylaid him, rehashing his story and query. Peets said he was rushing to get to the airport and handed Marcus his business card.

But yes, he had one possible contact to suggest. An American man by the name of Sweeney, living in Naples.

21

CENTRO STORICO

Carmela Zuccarello was staring into her plate of buffalo mozzarella, tomato, and basil, a colour scheme that echoed the flag of Italy. A flag drenched in olive oil — all the more authentic — which created a bubbling, swirling effect that resembled one of Kandinsky's less geometrical paintings. Having studied art history before switching to criminology, she was apt to wonder how different her life path could have been. At the moment, she was feeling tense, overworked, and overdue for a vacation, maybe one to a city with top-flight museums. The snow globes sitting on her shelf back at the office were a useful reminder of all the other places she could be.

In the meantime, getting away from the office meant a cheap but good restaurant a few blocks away. A screen mounted on the wall was playing an episode of *The Simpsons*. The restaurant cook wore a white cap and apron that matched the fluffy clouds pictured on the show. He slid pizzas into an oven clad in beige-and-white tiles that looked like seashells. Yet another hint that she needed that vacation. Her waiter refilled a glass of water using his good arm — the other was cradled in a sling. She didn't ask what had happened to him.

Zuccarello's phone rang — of course. It was impossible to take an actual lunch break longer than thirty-five minutes. It was the office receptionist, Sofia, relaying a phone message because it sounded important. A British man who worked in Naples but was currently in Los Angeles had information about the American murder victim. Zuccarello asked Sofia to text the man's name and phone number, and when it landed, she proceeded to search on her phone for the area code, which was not L.A. but U.K. She polished off what was left of her Kandinsky salad and paid the bill.

Outside on Vico D'Afflitto, she found a relatively quiet spot, leaned against a dilapidated wall, wished she had a cigarette, and dialed the number.

"Yes, thank you for calling back," said Professor David Brill. He explained in very serviceable, British-accented Italian that he was a *papirologo* based at Oxford who'd spent many years working with the papyri at the Officina. Brill had just been to an academic event in Los Angeles, where he heard some information pertinent to the death of Trevor Ballard.

"What can you tell me, Professor Brill?" said Zuccarello, switching to English.

"Well, the main piece of information that is possibly relevant is that Mr. Ballard had in his possession a papyrus scroll when he was killed."

A teenager on a motorcycle came to a stop and gunned the engine. Zuccarello frowned and walked in the opposite direction. "A papyrus scroll?" she said.

"Yes. It would appear that Mr. Ballard had been given a carbonized papyrus like those discovered at Herculaneum, the ones being studied in the Officina. And it disappeared after his, um, unfortunate death."

"How did you learn this, professor?"

"I heard about it yesterday from someone who was at the conference in Herculaneum, a Canadian man, who befriended Mr. Ballard and apparently loaned him the papyrus."

"I see. And the name of this Canadian man?"

"Sinclair. Marcus Sinclair. He himself inherited the papyrus from his uncle, who was a dealer in antiquities."

"Could you please text me the name of this man? And that of his uncle?"

"Yes, of course."

"And what is the significance here exactly?" Zuccarello asked. "Why do you think this papyrus is connected to Mr. Ballard's homicide?"

Brill cleared his throat. "I have no reason to think that per se," he said. "I just thought that the police should know. And — I don't mean to dwell on academic nuances — but there's reason to think that the papyrus in question contains material that was written by Julius Caesar. And that conceivably has value."

"Value? What sort of value?"

"Well, academic value, clearly. But such items can also have commercial value. And one other thing, if I may," Brill continued. "Tangential, perhaps, but a couple of months ago, when I was in Naples, my knapsack was stolen in the Spanish Quarter. A very long, detailed transcript of a papyrus I have been editing was in the knapsack. And, well . . ."

Yet another motorcycle drowned him out. Zuccarello had heard enough, anyway. Her text messages were chirping; she had to get back to the office and process all this. Brill was veering off topic. He was not the first tourist to have his bag lifted in the Quartieri Spagnoli. She wrapped things up. Brill said he might be back in Naples during the Christmas break.

Zuccarello walked briskly through a throng of shoppers at the Pignasecca market, the midday sunshine glinting off the silvery fish heaped in bins of ice. The place was a veritable seafood morgue.

This new information that Ballard had been in possession of a papyrus scroll dramatically altered the evidentiary picture. The victim's laptop and cell faded into the background and a small scroll was now in the spotlight. Was the artifact really worth anything? Was it worth killing a man for?

She passed a little square where a venerable olive tree stood, half its massive trunk growing out of a huge concrete planter. The silver-green leaves shimmered in the lunch-hour sunshine. She was reminded of Van Gogh's lyrical renderings of olive trees in the south of France. More vacation fantasies.

It was difficult to believe that those fusty academics — the Friends of Herculaneum, who gathered in Ercolano every two years, taking in the sights, sticking together like marmalade, scrambling around the sun-baked ruins — were involved in anything remotely lucrative.

Back at police headquarters, she breezed past security and hustled up the stairs to her office. She checked the file and saw that Marcus Sinclair had in fact been questioned by Giuseppe in the wake of Ballard's murder. However, Giuseppe's interview summary, half-assed as per usual, did not mention anything about a papyrus scroll. It did note that Sinclair had been among the very last people to see Ballard alive. Maybe the very last.

Sinclair had met Ballard at the Caffè Mexico on that last morning of his life. But a list of Ballard's credit card charges showed that he had lunch at Pizzeria Festa later that day. At least his last meal had been a good one; Festa was second to none for pizza. Could it be that Ballard had lunch with Sinclair? The substantial tab suggested a meal for two. And what about Sinclair's uncle, the antiquities dealer? How did he get his hands on a papyrus from Italy? Were those hands clean?

She phoned the Carabinieri for the Protection of Cultural Heritage, the art theft investigative unit, asking a colleague there to look into the uncle's background. Within hours she had her answer; the Carabinieri were able to pinpoint a half dozen items brokered by Gerald Sinclair that were of questionable provenance. Nothing major, the office hastened to add. Most international dealers had at least a few skeletons in their closet. Normally the Carabinieri wouldn't bother pursuing the matter, given the lack of hard evidence. But if she wanted grounds for a warrant, she had them.

Thus armed, Zuccarello prepared a warrant to seize one particular item acquired by Gerald Sinclair, a Roman amphora, as well as a subpoena for the questioning of Marcus Sinclair as a "person of interest" in the Ballard homicide. That would put the fear of God in the Canadian. He would have to appear either virtually or in person in Naples and answer some questions, chief among them questions about a papyrus scroll.

Zuccarello was well-versed about Rembrandt, Caravaggio, and Picasso. But papyri? The paper of antiquity never made it into her undergraduate classes. She tapped her password into her laptop; the machine shuddered to life, and she began searching online to educate herself on the subject. There was no shortage of material, rabbit hole leading to rabbit hole.

Clicking and reading, she was starting to appreciate why a papyrus scroll would be valued. The reason papyrus scrolls were so rarely found was that damp, whether coming from above ground or underground, destroyed them. There were two ways for papyri to survive. By staying dry, as happened in super-arid places like the Egyptian desert, or by being burned incompletely, as was the case in Herculaneum. After the eruption of Mount Vesuvius, the Herculaneum papyri ended up like toast left too long in the oven. Charred but not destroyed, they looked like lumps of charcoal. They were actually burned as fuel by the workers who first dug them up.

Good luck, she thought, trying to read the papyrus stolen from Ballard. But Professor Brill said it might have to do with Julius Caesar, that it could turn out to be a scholarship bonanza. So it was possible to decipher the thing? She read on and learned the history of various methods and their varied success; new digital technologies were now thought to improve the chances of decipherment.

The questions in Zuccarello's head were piling up, questions that she intended to put to Mr. Marcus Sinclair.

22

CHIAIA

Olivier Auger was in the *triclinium*, the dining room, seated on a Roman-style couch, one of three arrayed with classical authenticity in the shape of the Greek letter π. He braced himself for one of Sweeney's condescending lectures.

"Our archaeologist friends may have their heads in the sand, but they're not stupid," Sweeney said. "And they have found nothing new. Treasure hunters also have come up empty-handed. But is anyone really looking for papyrus scrolls? They've used everything from metal detectors to satellite technology to gauge whether any gold or bronze objects remain underground. I could care less for such things. The answer in any case seems to be no. But papyrus scrolls? Can there really be no other scrolls from Herculaneum floating around?"

"Apparently not," said Auger. "Except for the one in a little box. In Paris."

"Any progress on that front?"

"I am still working on the dossier," Auger said. "It is very difficult. The papyrus was a gift, you know, from the King of Naples to Napoleon Bonaparte. So it is part of France's national patrimony. And the Sorbonne? A bit like the Vatican."

Sweeney said, "I thought you were connected there?"

"Connected in the academic world, yes. But authorization for a precious item in the collection to be shipped away and subjected to a new technology? To achieve that, you need *political* connections."

Sweeney gave a sweeping motion with his hand, as if to dismiss something trivial. "Politics," he repeated under his breath. He adjusted a clasp in the form of an eagle that held together the upper folds of his toga-like smock.

The architecture, the furniture, the clothes, his vaunted Epicureanism — how much was for show? Or did they represent the true Thomas J. Sweeney? Auger couldn't say for certain, nor did he care. The dramatic creation of one's character was an art form unto itself. What mattered was that Sweeney was ruthless and brilliant and he understood technology. And he was rich.

"Think about it," Sweeney continued. "Some of the Herculaneum papyri are written in Latin, not just Greek. The Villa had to have had two libraries, Greek and Latin. That was standard then for Romans. I should have the same here," Sweeney added. "One day, perhaps."

"*Bien sûr* — there have to be more papyri underground."

Nonius appeared with a silver tray and two goblets of wine.

"*Gratias tibi.*" Sweeney's Italian was conspicuously bad, despite his having moved to Italy half a decade earlier. But he used every occasion to show off his mastery of Latin. More performance art?

Auger said, "And the Officina? There are so many unopened papyri, sitting in cabinets, doing nothing."

"You can't get within spitting distance of those scrolls without an alarm going off," Sweeney said. "Or without promising to spend a decade with an eye surgically attached to their microscopes. No offense, Olivier."

"I am not offended. I love my profession."

"Yes, you do. But you also love your lifestyle."

Auger did not register a hint of annoyance. "It is natural," he said. "I am close to my age of retirement."

They both fell silent and drank from their glasses.

"Your profession is indispensable," Sweeney continued. "But your methods take forever."

"My profession has the time."

Sweeney smiled. "Just keep doing what you've been doing," he said. "Get your name out there among the collectors. I can't be the only person able to see the forest for the papyri."

23

PALAZZO REALE

The statues of eight kings, carved from volcanic rock, illuminated by the southern Italian sunshine, were standing guard over a crime scene. That's how it looked to Kristi as she crossed the street from the café to the Piazza del Plebiscito and gazed at the Royal Palace. She unfolded a map indicating the palace's five entrances, its various gardens, the National Library, and the remote location of the Officina. She glanced around to get her bearings, paused, and inhaled the balmy air perfumed by the bay. Mindfulness was a therapeutic strategy but also a journalistic aid. In reportage, as in meditation, it was all about being aware, about noticing details.

On one side of the vast piazza was a sombre church flanked by curved colonnades. Two giant equestrian statues. Gaggles of tourists with selfie sticks. To her right was the Gambrinus and other cafés and restaurants at the foot of Via Toledo, the hubbub of the motorcycles and scooters and small cars zipping by with no shortage of drivers leaning on their horns. On her left was the bay dotted with sailboats oblivious to the brooding hulk of Vesuvius across the water.

She turned and walked toward the palace, scanning the giant statues of the monarchs who once ruled Naples. This was the sort of history she had time for: one thousand years of political rulers summed up in a two-minute walk. Marcus, the history prof, would not be impressed.

A mental game she played as a teenager came back. If she had to sleep with one of these monarchs, who would it be? Most — beginning with King Roger, who took power way back in 1132 — resembled scowling thugs. Victor Emmanuel II, with his sword pointing skywards, looked certifiably crazy. She opted for Charles VII, from the eighteenth century, a pensive-looking dreamer with cascades of curls that would not have appeared out of place on a heavy metal guitarist. He also kind of reminded her of Marcus.

Kristi returned her focus to the Royal Palace and, following her map, avoided the main entrance and continued past the stately opera house to the well-manicured park that was the Royal Gardens. Sunlight danced between the tree trunks. She passed a couple kissing and groping with gusto on a bench, averting her gaze though the image was burned onto her retina. A nice image. *Moving right along* — she actually mouthed those words to get her mind off the scene and continued toward the east side of the palace.

The signs were clear enough for Kristi to follow directions to the National Library. Once inside the building, she pretended to know where she was going and showed her ID at a security kiosk; she was assigned a locker for her knapsack and breezed through a turnstile with notepad, pen, and iPhone.

She climbed the double staircase leading to the Biblioteca Nazionale Vittorio Emanuele III, her eyes drawn to a vaulted ceiling with elaborate frescoes. Soon she was in the Sala di Lettura, the reading room, its carved bookshelves rising to a ceiling with white-and-gold bas-reliefs. Its dancing figures and musical themes contrasted with the silent, stationary readers below, who glanced up from their books and monitors as she strode by purposefully. Anyone watching would have assumed she knew where she was going. Kristi kept an eye out for directions to the Officina as she continued through rooms with ornate ceilings and towering bookshelves. Spines flashed powder-blue, khaki, or olive. A bust showed a grave-looking man with a droopy moustache. Another chamber was filled with old maps, panelled in dark wood, and a huge globe on bronze feet.

She passed a sign that declared, *ACCESSO RISERVATO AL PERSONALE DELLA BIBLIOTECA.*

In a narrow hallway, she noticed another sign: *SEZIONE PAPIRI,* the papyrus section. She entered a narrow corridor flanked by high bookshelves resembling the tottering tenements of the Spanish Quarter. Then a sign, *ATTENTI ALLA TESTA,* warned those entering a weirdly small archway to duck.

The archway joined a narrow hallway that brought her into a spacious room with a framed floor plan of the Villa dei Papiri on one wall. Posters for academic symposia. Tall bookcases. A bust which by now she easily recognized as Epicurus. In the middle of the room was a rectangle of blond wooden desks, each holding a microscope. The only person at work was a youngish man with a short haircut and eyeglasses with chunky lenses. He glanced up from his microscope to look in her direction.

She'd arrived. This was the nerve centre that had loomed so large in her thoughts these past months: the Officina dei Papiri Ercolanesi.

"Posso aiutarla?"

A librarian in high heels was carrying a board that contained what looked like swirls of Nutella. Kristi knew what it was: a sheet of papyrus that had been unrolled, cut, and fastened to a stiff cardboard backing. But she couldn't make sense of the Italian being spoken to her. The woman carrying the papyrus sheet switched to English.

"Might I help you?"

Kristi had prepared her response in advance: she was looking for an academic publication called *Cronache Ercolanesi*.

The librarian pursed her lips, puzzled, and walked over to a nearby bookshelf, asking in broken English more than once for the name of that journal. "*Io non parlo bene l'italiano*," Kristi said, apologetically. She repeated the name *Cronache Ercolanesi*. The library didn't have it, which made no sense, as it was the main academic journal about the Herculaneum scrolls.

The man with chunky eyeglasses walked over stiffly and said "Cronache," pronouncing the "che" as a hard *k*. Kristi had been pronouncing the "che" like Che Guevara. The Italian woman threw up her arms in a hallelujah gesture. Kristi smiled sheepishly, apologized to the librarian and thanked the man.

"Are you a papyrologist?" he asked with a German accent, beads of moisture above his upper lip.

"Oh, not at all. I'm a journalist. Researching the scrolls."

"You are writing an article?"

"Yes. For the *Toronto Star*. In Canada."

"Ah, okay. Ask me if you require any more help," he said.

"Thanks! I may take you up on that."

Kristi pulled out a few volumes of *Cronache Ercolanesi* and set them on the table. She had no desire to read more of the turgid academic journal she'd already struggled with in Toronto. Instead, her eyes scanned the layout of the Officina, trying to pinpoint where the scrolls were stored.

THE YOUNG MAN, Christoph Hirshleifer, was having trouble focusing on his papyrus fragment. The Officina attracted few visitors, and the Canadian journalist was pretty in a way he'd imagined his future wife to be. True, she was older than him. But maturity was something he felt drawn to. The women of Naples seemed like girls to him. Attractive, sure, vivacious, but somehow insubstantial, not to mention never giving him the time of day. That he got around town on a bicycle did not seem to help his cause.

He leaned into the binocular microscope, studying the damaged Greek letters of a Philodemus tract. It was titled *On Vices and Their Corresponding Virtues*. But the text no longer resembled anything, black splotches swimming in his distracted mind. He considered approaching the journalist. The Officina was his sphere of interest. If he couldn't interest a woman curious about papyri, who could he interest? But the mere thought was generating anxiety.

The decision was made for him. "Excuse me," Kristi said. "Sorry to disturb you. But would you be able to tell me where the papyri are kept?"

"Um, yes," Christoph said. He powered off the microscope, got to his feet, happy to stretch his long legs again. "But you must request access to them by filling in an Officina application form. And only accredited scholars can make the request."

"Of course. I understand. I just want to be able to describe where they are."

"Okay. I will show you."

Christoph led Kristi to an adjacent room filled with dozens of gunmetal filing cabinets. Were it not for some vitrines displaying carbonized lumps of papyrus, it could have passed as a locker room.

"Here it is," he said.

Another small bust of Epicurus loomed over one of the cabinets where Christoph slid open a drawer. He pulled out a sheet of papyrus on a cardboard backing.

"PHerc 817, for example," Christoph said. "That's the catalogue number. All the papyri from the Villa are numbered like this."

"Wow," Kristi said, happy to have found someone to talk to. "What's this papyrus about?"

"It's actually one of the most interesting papyri," piped in another man, who was on the far side of the room. "It tells the story of the

Battle of Actium." He slid shut a file drawer. "When Octavian defeated Marco Antonio and Cleopatra. And who are you?"

"Kristi Grainger. I'm a journalist. From Toronto."

"You are writing about the Officina?"

"She's researching the papyri," said Christoph curtly. "It is a poem," he added.

The other scholar introduced himself as Lorenzo. "The poem says," he said, "that Cleopatra had many criminals killed with different kinds of poison, and other ways, so she could know what kind of suicide would be not so painful for her."

"That's pretty grisly," said Kristi.

"It's actually very beautiful," said Christoph softly. "It is written in Latin that is very poetic. Only about fifty lines have survived."

"That we have here," said Lorenzo. "One part was given to Napoleon Bonaparte and has disappeared. So who knows what may be hiding in Paris? Or" — he circled the air with his free hand — "in one of these cabinets."

24

CENTRO STORICO

He was half expecting — dreading, really — the Italian authorities to make inquiries about his scroll. He'd been upfront about lending Ballard the papyrus when questioned by Naples police after the man's murder. So it wasn't a total surprise when Marcus returned home from L.A. to find a letter from the Pubblica Sicurezza seeking information about Gerald's collection of antiquities.

What did surprise him was that the Italian investigation focused on one item and one item only: an amphora vividly decorated with a black-figured Hercules slaying a minotaur. This was, in fact, the Roman jug that once contained Gerald's papyrus. But the scroll itself was apparently irrelevant to the authorities.

The amphora was now sitting in an evidence locker at RCMP headquarters in Ottawa; as advised, he had turned it over to Canadian police. According to the warrant, the amphora had been looted by tomb raiders in the Campania region during the 1970s. It had since been in the possession of one Giacomo Pagani, an Italian art dealer convicted of conspiracy to traffic in antiquities. Evidence included Polaroid photos seized from Pagani's storehouse in Geneva, Switzerland, one showing the amphora still encrusted with dirt. Gerald had supposedly purchased it from Pagani for $40,000.

Did that mean his uncle's business dealings were less than kosher? The notion had certainly been percolating in his head. Going through Gerald's papers, he was struck by the amount of opaque information, the unprovenanced items, the references to a "private Swiss collector," and the Rolodex containing less-than-specific names such as "Italian dealer" and "Giacomo" (presumably the aforementioned Pagani).

The idea of going back to Italy filled him with both buoyancy and trepidation. Ballard was dead. His own hotel room had been ransacked. And Naples was Naples. Yet Kristi was there. What's more, he now had a lead courtesy of Connor Peets and the Holy Books Foundation. A fierce, unlikely determination was growing ever stronger within him to track down the scroll.

Not long after unpacking his bag from California, Marcus repacked it for Italy. His carry-on held one unusual item: a segment of a papyrus scroll, glued to a board and fitted inside a plastic container Laszlo had crafted.

Marcus flew to Frankfurt and from there to Naples. As he rode the airport escalator, his tired eyes were drawn to gigantic black-and-white ads for an Italian men's clothing line, dapper 007-type men with tag lines in English like "A Gentleman Finds Irony in Everything." Another ad for the same company declared: "A Gentleman Knows What She Likes." Marcus's mind free-associated to Kristi. What *did* she like? Marcus didn't even own a suit. A sports jacket over a polo shirt and jeans, his current attire, was as "gentlemanly" as he got.

He glanced around, looking for taxi signage. On a screen, arrival times flashed for flights from Milano, Olbia, Nice, Roma, and London. A faux-Roman bust at a cruise ship kiosk looked entirely convincing.

And a lonely piano stood against one wall, waiting for a virtuoso with a delayed flight to play it.

Marcus noticed with surprise a corner of the terminal decorated in scenes from Pompeii and Herculaneum: floor-to-ceiling reproductions of wall paintings from the Vesuvian cities. And young travellers were lounging on ersatz ancient Roman couches in what was billed as a "*Triclinium*," helpfully translated into English as "Lunch in a Pompeii Home." A showcase contained vases and glassware designed to resemble — for all he knew, maybe they were authentic? — antiquities.

Soon he was at a taxi stand, from which he could actually see the double humps of Mount Vesuvius. And not too long afterward, he was at the Hotel Palazzo Cardo. After making sure to fasten the chain on his door, he slept a bit, fitfully, but awoke in the early evening. After a couple of excellent pizza slices from Sorbillo, a famed spot nearby, he underwent a sleepless night due to jittery nerves and haywire circadian rhythms.

Daytime brought his first order of business at the Naples police building. Carmela Zuccarello was smooth, courteous, and elegant. That was Italy for you. Even the garbage men were outfitted in stylish coveralls that might have figured in a glossy magazine spread. Whether Naples deserved its reputation for sinking under mountains of garbage was another matter. So far as Marcus could see, the city adequately cleaned up after itself.

Zuccarello's office was immaculate, everything in its place. Even a collection of snow globes was attractively arrayed, not unlike Zuccarello herself, with her pageboy hair and curvy figure. The snow globes seemed like a quirky decor for a no-nonsense homicide cop. After a cursory greeting, she got straight to the point.

"Do you know where your uncle got this amphora?"

"'Private collection' is how it's listed," Marcus replied. "I'm still going through his record-keeping system, which is not so easy for me to understand."

"Private collection," repeated Zuccarello, jotting something down on a pad.

A colleague knocked at her door and came in, the same detective who questioned Marcus after Ballard was killed. He looked less sleepy and bored than the previous time around.

"I believe you have met Giuseppe before," Zuccarello said. The detective, in a crisp blue shirt and two-day-old stubble, nodded to Marcus and took a seat.

"We are waiting for your police to send the amphora to us," Zuccarello continued. "Apparently it's quite beautiful. Did you not realize that it was something of great value?"

"It's not my area of specialization. More often than not I can't tell the difference between something very valuable and something that's not worth much." A case in point, he thought, was Gerald's scroll. Which just happened to have been stashed by his uncle in the amphora. He saw no reason to specify that the amphora had housed a papyrus scroll.

"Do not Canadian authorities require provenance certification after someone dies?"

Where is she going with this line of questioning? he wondered.

"I had all the main items in his collection professionally evaluated. I had to; there were capital gains taxes to be paid. The amphora — my uncle used it as a night table with a lamp on it! — was evaluated. Its value was $5,000, not a crazy amount."

"You don't find $250,000 U.S. a crazy amount?"

"What? That sounds incredible to me. Is that what you think it's worth?"

"That's what our art squad experts are saying," she said.

Giuseppe chimed in: "Depending on the age of the amphora."

"I believe it's first century after Christ. That's from the insurance policy information."

A motorcycle roared from somewhere outside the office window, a window which showed only the brickwork of the adjacent building, the sort of view a prisoner gets to see.

"Could you forward us the evaluation you received?"

"Sure. Of course."

Zuccarello got out of her chair and walked over to the bookcase, the one with the snow globes. "I'm also told that you were close friends with Trevor Ballard at the conference?"

"Yes, well, just for a few days during the conference and a bit after. Until Trevor's death. I was devastated by what happened."

"And you apparently gave him a papyrus from Herculaneum that disappeared?"

"Lent it to him, yes. I explained that when I was questioned." He looked at the cop named Giuseppe, who nodded. His hopes to retrieve the scroll suddenly surged. The police were now involved. "Have you by any chance found it?"

She ignored his question and returned to her sparse desk, leafing through a file folder. "And apparently an Italian physicist was somehow involved with Mr. Ballard. Can you tell me about your contact with him?"

Marcus shifted in the hard-backed chair. He felt exhausted; his eyelids might have been weighed down with lead. He had good reason to tell the police everything he knew about the scroll. But he'd promised Kristi that he'd keep the Italian scientist's identity under wraps as a journalistic source. Yet here he was in a foreign country being grilled by police about a murder.

"Um, his first name is Antonio," Marcus said. "I believe he lives here in Naples. But that's all I know. Trevor apparently met him a couple of times."

"And," she said, "can you remind us where you were on the afternoon Mr. Ballard died?"

"I was at the hotel. Or near the hotel, outside."

Giuseppe said, "The hotel where Ballard was killed?"

"Yes. Well, not at that exact time. I mean, I don't know exactly when everything happened."

"When what happened?" Giuseppe again, more gruffly.

It was hot inside the small room, no air con.

"I mean, I don't know anything about what happened," Marcus said. "I was down the street at a store buying a bottle of water when the ambulance arrived. I heard the sirens."

"And," Giuseppe said, "you could know the *ambulanza* was for your friend?"

"Um, I didn't know at first. But Olivier Auger, you know, the professor from France, I crossed paths with him outside a few hours later and he told me."

Marcus felt the back of his neck getting warm and an itch on the left side of his face.

"Auger?"

"Olivier Auger. He's one of the papyrologists. He was also at the conference."

Zuccarello sat back down at her desk and jotted down some notes on a yellow pad. Giuseppe said nothing, looking pleased with himself. Marcus folded his arms, which formed a kind of security blanket for him. He had nothing to hide. So why was he feeling sweaty and stressed? He unfolded his arms and said, "Look, I could have been the victim here. My hotel room was ransacked. Someone was looking for something."

"Ransacked?"

"Yes. Someone broke into the hotel room and searched through my things, leaving everything upside down."

Zuccarello wanted to know why he hadn't mentioned this before. "This is significant," she said.

"It only happened the night before I left. I'd already been questioned." He looked from Zuccarello to Giuseppe. "I was afraid.

I wasn't going to delay my flight to report something that may have been nothing."

"You were afraid," said Giuseppe, "of something that was nothing?"

Marcus had no answer to that.

"Was there anything stolen?" Zuccarello asked.

"No. Nothing was stolen. I was shaken up. My friend at the conference had just been killed in the same hotel."

She spent a few silent minutes flipping through her notes. Finally, Zuccarello looked up. "Thank you for meeting us here," she said. "We could have set up a video conference call, but that's never as good as talking in person. You can email the amphora evaluation to my office. Please call me if you think of anything else that might be useful to our investigation. I hope you can enjoy your time in Naples now that you're here again."

AN HOUR OR SO LATER, Marcus exited the five-star Hotel Palazzo Cardo, a haven of luxury on a bleak side street. He thought of the last hotel he'd stayed at in Naples, the one where Ballard was killed and his own space was invaded. He knew that Kristi was planning to go there to try to pry information from hotel staff. Perhaps he could join her. Or maybe that would be pushing his luck; he felt more fearful than he'd expected being back in Naples.

The city was not built for automobiles; in the Centro Storico, the downtown core, cars were shoehorned into whatever space remained free; in his present whereabouts, that meant smack in front of the hotel's entrance. Neighbouring buildings had laundry hanging perilously low from windows, and violent swirls of graffiti scrawled on every available bare wall.

His mind drifted back to Kristi. She was staying at an Airbnb nearby, and they had plans to meet up that evening. But she sounded busy when he texted her. His single status was often the result of calculating all the possible things that might go wrong with potential partners. *But I have to change*, he told himself. *I will change. The time has come.* He'd heard this monologue before, only it was louder now.

He walked up a little hill to the Spaccanapoli, that animated street that had been there since the city was called "Neapolis." His heart skipped a few beats when a Polizia Municipale car slammed to a halt in front of him and a cop emerged. But it wasn't what he momentarily feared — his own arrest. The officer had simply stopped to chat with an acquaintance.

Marcus had the odd sensation that he was being followed, and he ducked into Bar Nilo, a coffee shop that served booze. Inside he sipped a bittersweet macchiato and studied a mini-shrine to Diego Maradona behind the counter. Pictures of the soccer legend feinting and dancing around hapless defenders loomed over bottles of Peroni and Lacryma Christi.

Back outside on the Spaccanapoli, he found himself face to face with a statue of a reclining Nile river god. Its head had famously been decapitated, stolen, and returned more than once. A woman in a window three stories up lowered a huge bowl hanging from a rope till it landed in the hands of a young man who placed a package inside. As she hoisted it up to her window, he thought of Laszlo trying to unroll Gerald's papyrus on the Piaggio machine. An old man in a grimy undershirt craned his neck out another window. An attractive woman wearing large sunglasses dragged a rolling suitcase along the cobblestones, producing a *clackety-clack* rhythm as she turned off the street and into the Santa Maria Assunta dei Pignatelli church. Welcome to Naples, a mashup of Maradona and Madonna.

A teenager zipped by on a scooter with a dog tucked snugly into her sweatshirt. A stream of motorcycles then passed by so closely that he felt ripples of air on his forearm. The theft of Brill's knapsack came to mind, and Marcus tightened the straps on his own. He checked

Google Maps, hoping to make it on foot to the next meeting on his itinerary. But he quickly realized he needed a taxi. He had that first segment of the scroll in his knapsack and the address of Thomas J. Sweeney.

25

CHIAIA

The taxi drove through the Chiaia neighbourhood, passing a long waterfront park, fashionably dressed women with outsized shopping bags, and swanky boutiques. Soon Marcus was standing outside an elegant palazzo where a muscular Italian man with chiselled features answered the door and led him inside, past whitewashed walls eerily lined with masks, a dazzling atrium with a pool, and then a reception room decorated with marble walls and mosaics.

Thomas Sweeney, sitting on a couch, put down the tablet he'd been reading.

"Sinclair the Younger!" He raised a palm by way of greeting but remained seated and made no effort to shake hands. Sweeney was wearing a Mao-collared smock and oval glasses. His white hair, what remained of it, was combed tightly back.

"Welcome to my little corner of antiquity," he said.

"Wow," Marcus said. "Some of this stuff should be in a public museum."

"I don't believe in public museums," Sweeney said.

They engaged in small talk about Italy, during which Sweeney explained that he'd moved from "one Bay area to another" — San Francisco to Naples — after going into "virtual retirement." He said that he had known Gerald well. He'd purchased several artifacts with Gerald's help a long time ago while still living in California. They'd even played tennis together.

"Wicked serve your uncle had. But I've stopped playing; it's brutal on the old knees. So you won't get revenge for Gerald on the clay court if that's what you're here for."

"No worries. I did not bring my tennis racquet."

"Oh, we're all of us in one kind of racket or another."

Marcus searched his mind for a clever response but drew a blank. For the second time that day, his meeting with Zuccarello being the first, he fought back a wave of fatigue that left his brain sloshing around without moorings. Jet lag was kicking in.

All at once, the whole exercise felt futile. So much trouble for some shrivelled book from antiquity. But the historian in him couldn't resist the idea that twenty centuries ago, someone went to the trouble of forming words with a quill or a split reed using ink made from carbon mixed with gum and water. And a volcanic freak of nature combined with a lucky discovery and an enigmatic uncle had all conspired to place those words in his possession. He wanted the scroll back. Or at the very least, he needed to learn why it had been stolen.

Marcus had been vague when he first contacted Sweeney, saying only that he had an artifact from Gerald that he could use some help figuring out. He now dipped into his backup energy reserve to explain what led him to Naples.

"I don't have Gerald's tennis skills, though he did teach me how to play. However, I did inherit some interesting things from my uncle." He recounted the amphora, the papyrus, the Piaggio machine, and the impasse with an unyielding scroll, a scroll that had disappeared right here in Naples. All that remained was the segment that Laszlo had unrolled, cut, and glued to a board. He had that with him in his knapsack.

Sweeney's cat-like eyes widened. He didn't move a muscle, though, and remained sitting very still. If a limestone Sphinx from the Egyptian desert were to come to life, Marcus thought it would resemble this man.

"Indeed," Sweeney said softly. "I would love to have a look."

Marcus carefully opened the plastic case to reveal the charred segment in a foam frame. Placed on a marble table with elaborately carved legs, the carbonized sheet of papyrus looked even more underwhelming than usual.

Sweeney leaned so close to the papyrus that it seemed he was trying to inhale a subterranean stench seventeen hundred years in the making.

"Any idea," Marcus asked, "how I might be able to find the scroll this came from?"

Sweeney lifted his head from the papyrus. "Remarkable," he said. "As it happens, I've been researching this sort of issue extensively." He paused. "I can perhaps make inquiries about tracking down this lost scroll. I may even have a method of locating it."

"Really? How would you do it?"

Sweeney reached for a bowl of mints and unwrapped one. "You'll have to pardon a certain amount of science here. Finding out what papyrus fragments and pieces belong together is not as easy as one might imagine."

He popped the mint in his mouth.

"The so-called experts, the papyrologists, hold scraps of papyrus — like yours here — in the air, shifting them to allow the light to glance off them from different angles. It helps them make out the writing."

Sweeney's assistant appeared, poured two glasses of wine, added water, and exchanged what looked to be a meaningful glance with his employer. Marcus was taken aback, then told himself that being back in Italy was stirring up irrational worries.

"Papyrologists are aided by other equipment like binocular microscopes and multi-spectral imaging. But we've made scant progress since Piaggio invented his traction machine two centuries ago. The goal is to see more of a contrast between the ink and the papyrus. Which isn't easy. It's like trying to read a burnt newspaper."

Marcus recalled the black powder that flaked off Gerald's scroll when he first touched it.

Sweeney continued, "The greater challenge is to read a papyrus that cannot be physically unrolled, like the one you lost. A few years ago, the first attempts were made using medical X-rays. Unfortunately, the exercise was a failure despite a huge expenditure of time, labour, and equipment. The main difficulty was that the ink and the papyrus it was written on both absorbed X-rays in precisely the same way.

"Enter a new technological method I have pioneered. My solution uses X-rays from a synchrotron radiation facility, which reveal enough contrast between ink and papyrus, enough of a difference in the landscape of the scroll, that it can actually be read."

"I've heard something about that. What exactly is a synchrotron?"

"It's a special type of particle accelerator. Basically, it propels electrons to near light speed."

Sweeney offered Marcus a mint from the bowl on his side table. Marcus felt hunger mixed with jet lag and some difficulty staying focused on the nuances of the technology. He took a mint and slowly unwrapped it.

"So we scan a papyrus scroll," Sweeney said, "using X-ray phase-contrast tomography. And the next step, where I come in really, is to apply specialized software and machine-learning to detect the carbon-based ink, which takes the form of something called 'crackle,' a sort of fracturing in the shape of the ink. This crackle in the ink is different enough from the papyrus for my software to detect that difference. The software then sifts through the jumbled layers of letters and makes sense of them. I call it virtual unwrapping."

Marcus said, "It sounds almost too good to be true. But how does this technology help me find my missing scroll?"

"It's not a slam dunk," the old man said. "And it will take some research. But I'm more than happy to help Gerald Sinclair's nephew. A papyrus scroll like the one your uncle somehow procured cannot stay under wraps for long, even though it's not exactly a lost Caravaggio painting. In fact, it's of no value to anyone unless it is deciphered."

"So what do you propose to do?"

"Give me — by that, of course, I mean *lend me* — this sheet of papyrus, and I will try to find a match based on what has been circulating on the market and, perhaps, what has been submitted to scanning facilities. There has to be a paper trail. I don't need it for long, and I will get it back to you intact, fingers crossed, with the papyrus it came from. *If* we're fortunate. And you know what they say — fortune favours the bold."

26

CENTRO STORICO

Zuccarello took the stairs up to the police canteen. Not so long ago, she'd have stopped in the stairwell to smoke a cigarette, the better to disentangle the threads of a case. That's how something developed with Giuseppe, who was always only too happy to light up. She nixed the habit — both habits! — with an ease that was surprising to her. But there were times when either indulgence would have come in handy. Like right now; she could use some nicotine to help puzzle out the interview with Marcus Sinclair.

The canteen was empty aside from one table occupied by a few plainclothes cops deep in conversation. One of them noticed the homicide chief, straightened his posture and said hello. Two other heads swivelled in her direction. She gave a small wave as if she were busy, which she was, and headed for the vending machines. How pathetic it was to procure espresso from a machine when there was no shortage of high-calibre cafés right outside the building. But she needed to think things through without distraction.

Marcus Sinclair seemed highly unlikely to be the perpetrator of Ballard's murder. Why would he need to steal his own scroll? Yet instinct told her that he was concealing something. The questions about his uncle's amphora struck a nerve. Why? Probably the elder Sinclair had been an antiquities merchant who looted the hell out of Italy.

Zuccarello slid a euro into the machine, and a plastic cup descended to the robotic sound of clicks and gears. Marcus had also seemed to dissemble about the Italian physicist. She'd ask Giuseppe to check the university and science institutes for a physics expert named Antonio.

She removed the cup of subpar coffee from the vending machine. And another thing, that scholar Auger, who Marcus said first notified him about Ballard's murder. She'd have to figure out the Frenchman's whereabouts and verify his story. How did Auger get wind of Ballard's murder so early on?

She made her way to a table at the other end of the canteen, the three cops flashing smiles, flirting maybe, or more likely worried that the homicide chief would join them and assign actual work. Sitting alone, one hand wrapped around the plastic cup, she took stock of the Ballard case. Auger, check. The physicist, check. That left one other loose thread: Sinclair's hotel room break-in. What was the point of that? She needed to confirm whether it in fact happened two days after Ballard was killed. Logic dictated that whoever murdered Trevor Ballard, or whoever ordered the murder, knew that the scroll came from Sinclair. The same logic meant that whoever rifled through the luggage was hoping to find something else, perhaps something related to the scroll, in Sinclair's hotel room.

Was the theft of Professor Brill's knapsack related? It was as if there was a bounty on papyrus scrolls.

Another person of interest was that eccentric American entrepreneur who evidently felt his wealth placed him above the law in Italy. He'd ignored her request for detailed information about his meetings with Ballard. Yet he must have known that Ballard had a papyrus scroll. If anyone was bent on somehow monetizing the Herculaneum ruins and scrolls, it was Mr. Sweeney. She would have a subpoena prepared and sent to the palazzo of Thomas Sweeney.

Zuccarello drained the remaining coffee. Truth be told, it wasn't half bad, and it helped her think things through. If only it were a Turkish coffee. There were no dregs at the bottom of the cup, nothing she could easily decipher.

27

PIAZZA BELLINI

The Officina closed its doors mid-afternoon, forcing an end to the on-site papyrus lesson Kristi was getting from Christoph Hirshleifer and Lorenzo Clemente. But the two scholars were happy to keep chatting with a vivacious journalist who appeared to be actually interested in their rarefied field of study. So they left the National Library together and walked up to Piazza Bellini for coffee.

Along the way, Kristi learned more about papyrology than she cared to know. It sounded even more tedious than she had assumed, the contents of the scrolls even more arcane. She was at a loss to understand why anyone living in a seaside city as alluring as Naples would spend so much time cooped up indoors studying the burnt fragments of ancient books.

They found seats at a café table in the piazza, shade trees overhead. Violin scales from the nearby music conservatory drifted through the air along with a pungent whiff of hashish. A few metres away lay ruins from twenty-five hundred years earlier, when the city was a Greek colony, ruins that struck Kristi as little more than a hole in the ground.

They ordered coffee and agreed to share a pizza. Lorenzo removed a joint from a pack of cigarettes with the Fortuna label. He quickly slid it in and out of his mouth to moisten it, lit a match, and inhaled deeply. He let the smoke fill his lungs and exhaled a thin stream of grey.

"You know how the margherita pizza was created?" he asked. "The Queen of Italy in eighteen hundred something, Queen Margherita, was visiting Naples and went to the Pizzeria Brandi," Lorenzo said.

"Which still exists near the Officina," Christoph added. "Facing the Piazza del Plebiscito."

"So," Lorenzo continued, "the chef, a famous pizza chef, did a special thing. He made a pizza with the colours of the Italian flag to honour her. He took the red from the tomato, the white from the mozzarella, and green from basil."

"Nice," said Kristi. "Everything here is so beautiful. The architecture, the fashion, the cars, and the food, of course."

Lorenzo leaned back, tilting his chair with him. He had a mop of dark brown hair, a square jaw, and black, horn-rimmed glasses. "The papyri are a window for history," he said.

"From what I've seen," Kristi said, "that window has a pretty limited view. What's been deciphered so far is mostly about the Epicureans versus the Stoics."

"That's the content of a lot of the scrolls, true," Christoph said. "But only the scrolls that have been opened."

"Which is only like the amount of milk in a cappuccino," Lorenzo said. "Three hundred papyri have not been opened. Or more."

Christoph said, "That's because all the scrolls that can be unrolled have been unrolled. All the remaining ones are impossible to open."

"Except," Lorenzo said, "for the papyri underground in the Villa. Waiting for excavation."

The two men seemed to be vying for her attention. Kristi was accustomed to that. Lorenzo outclassed his friend in most respects. Even his academic area of specialty — the fall of the Roman Republic — was more compelling than Christoph's study of Philodemus. Dark-eyed and quick to smile, Lorenzo moved gracefully, in contrast to Christoph's awkwardness.

Christoph had short-cropped sandy-brown hair and was wearing a button-down shirt. He shifted his frame with effort, as if his legs were too long for the seat. He was in Naples on a post-doc fellowship from the Giambattista Vico Foundation; Professor Brill was his academic advisor. The grant would run out in a year, and Christoph admitted he was anxious about landing an academic appointment at a German classics department. A career in accounting, which he'd also studied at the undergraduate level, would be a crushing defeat for him, "like taking one of Cleopatra's poisons," he said.

Kristi flashed a thin smile.

Lorenzo's academic situation was no more secure. He had yet to make his mark by editing a papyrus scroll or publishing his dissertation. And standing out in the field of Late Republican Roman studies was no small task in Italy.

Kristi had stalled as long as she could and finally uttered the question uppermost in her mind. "Did you guys know Trevor Ballard?"

Christoph said, "We saw him once."

"Really? Where?"

"Vesuvius. We climbed the mountain with delegates from the conference."

"That's on my to-do list," Kristi said. "Hiking Vesuvius."

Lorenzo cupped his hand that held the burning joint to Kristi, and angled his head to Christoph, saying, "I know he doesn't want any."

"No thanks," she said, glancing around to see if anyone cared or even took notice of the hash smoke. Nobody seemed to.

She asked them, "What was Ballard like? Did he have anything interesting to say?"

"Ballard wanted to know information about the papyrus scrolls," Lorenzo said, exhaling smoke with a wince. "Basic stuff."

"We weren't actually at the conference," Christoph added. "Just joined the group for the day at Vesuvius. He spoke to Professor Auger a lot. About the papyri."

Kristi said, "About deciphering the papyri?"

"About virtual unrolling," Christoph said.

"The magic solution," said Lorenzo. "Myself, I will not be holding my breath for it to happen."

He took another drag, held it in, and blew out a cloud of smoke.

28

MATERDEI

It seemed almost too easy, as if his uncle had left a trail of crumbs for Marcus to follow. Sweeney hinted strongly that the lost papyrus could be tracked down and the mystery of its contents revealed. Gerald's scroll would come full circle, in Naples. And Marcus could preside over the cracking of its code, even study the text, with help of a papyrologist, and eventually publish something truly scholarly for the first time in his life.

He walked from Sweeney's home in upscale Chiaia to the gritty Spanish Quarter, full of dilapidated buildings seemingly on the verge of collapse. The early-evening sky was fading to purple-grey. An abandoned, gutted building had layer upon layer of graffiti on its windows and interior walls. Somehow it reminded him of the overlapping, rolled-up pages of a papyrus.

Gerald had urged him to "follow the trail of the papyrus," and he had. Might this be the end of the road for his scroll? The notion filled

Marcus with melancholy, though he wasn't sure why. Had he been clinging to the papyrus even when he lost it? Projecting his thwarted aspirations onto it, maybe? Hoping it would somehow give his life more purpose?

He avoided the squatters across the street from the National Archaeological Museum and ventured up Toledo toward the Materdei district. As he climbed the steep hill in waning light, he had the sense that he was witnessing, despite the droning motorbikes, a very old culture, as old as ancient Rome, or even older. He'd read about quarrying here by people who predated the Greeks. Beneath the cobbles of Naples was a labyrinth of catacombs, sewers, cisterns, ossuaries, and crypts going back seven thousand years.

Headlights from a passing motorbike danced on the stone walls, illuminating swirls of graffiti. Had he veered off track and gotten lost in the darkness? It wasn't meant to be such a long walk to the restaurant. He should have cabbed it. To calm his jangled nerves, he tried to imagine the street by day. Nighttime was playing tricks and fear probably distorted everything. A man wearing dark glasses stopped him to ask for money. Marcus fished a coin out of his pocket and picked up his pace, passing an elderly woman sitting in a wheelchair at the edge of a building. Was she begging too? Even the plaster statuettes of saints seemed to be beseeching in the feeble light that flickered from wall shrines.

Time was proceeding slower than usual. He recalled the memory of a wrong turn taken one time in Sao Paulo. He couldn't say what specifically was the risk — then or now — but something in the atmosphere, something in the faces of people, signalled grave danger. A panic button deep in the core of his body was activated. That old fear. What had Epicurus written somewhere about mortality? *We all live in a city without walls.*

Finally, in the distance, he could make out a small neon sign and dozens of people. He had made it to his destination: Festa pizzeria. There had really been nothing to worry about.

The pizzeria dominated a chaotic intersection with people filing in and shouting, smoking, leaning on scruffy masonry while motorbikes weaved through the crowd. Marcus joined the lineup, gave his name to a woman with a clipboard, then stood on the cobblestones with fifty other people. Every minute or so, a booming loudspeaker blared the name of someone on the waiting list.

After his name was announced he entered Festa, where he was given a plastic card with a table number on it and followed a waiter through a brick archway to another room, and in turn to another, and yet another. He was seated at table 29.

Marcus ordered the Pizza del Papa, which Festa invented for Pope John Paul II, who, according to the English menu, blessed pizza-makers during a visit to Naples. A Napoli-Palermo soccer match was being broadcast on a wall-mounted television screen, drawing anxious glances from the swift, dexterous waiters.

When it arrived, the Pizza del Papa was a thin-crusted triumph of butternut squash cream, zucchini flowers, roasted peppers, and smoked mozzarella. Festa was the highest rated pizzeria in Naples, and that was saying something. Marcus ate the pizza in rapture, his eyes drawn to both the soccer match and the framed photos of Sophia Loren. In the movie *L'Oro di Napoli*, the local icon had made pizzas and lost a ring; the black-and-white pictures showed her in a sensual dough-making pose.

He remembered that Trevor was greatly amused by his calculation that the temperature of a pizza oven — four hundred degrees Celsius — was more or less the same as that generated by a volcanic eruption like the one that fried the Herculaneum papyri. And, Marcus grimly reminded himself, this was where Trevor Ballard had eaten his last meal.

29

HOTEL PALAZZO CARDO

An hour later, Marcus was sitting in the dimly lit hotel bar, comparing notes with Kristi. He'd taken a taxi back from the pizzeria. The walk to the restaurant had been sufficiently unnerving; he had no desire to risk it again at such a late hour. Plus he was exhausted; in the last seventy-two hours, he'd slept for no more than ten in a few installments, on two planes, one taxi, and on an uncomfortably soft hotel mattress.

"The homicide chief let it slip that Ballard had lunch at Festa the day he died. So I went there to check it out."

She sipped prosecco; he drank fizzy water.

"How did they figure out where Ballard ate?"

"Not sure. A meal receipt, I think. The info just popped out when they were questioning me. Actually, it was Zuccarello's junior who let it slip. The detective who questioned me last time around, after Ballard was killed. She shut him down today with a look."

"I still can't get my head around this," Kristi said. "Why would a letter written by Julius Caesar two thousand years ago get anyone killed today?"

"Money? Academic rivalries? A Caesarian secret society?"

"I was talking about it with Christoph and Lorenzo. Not about the Caesar scroll — they didn't mention it, so presumably they're not aware of its existence. Just about Herculaneum scrolls in general. They didn't know much about Ballard, only briefly met him."

Someone was improvising on a piano that sat in the corner of the bar. Meanwhile, the sound system was piping in "So What" by Miles Davis. Was the freelance pianist trying to play along? Marcus found it jarring.

He said, "Do you think they're hiding something?"

"I doubt it. They didn't mention any new scroll, so neither did I. But from what they said, your scroll would be worth a lot of money, for sure. They mentioned a papyrus fragment of the Gospel of John that sold for $400,000 a decade ago. They both knew about this, despite having their heads in the academic clouds."

"So heads in the clouds but feet on the ground?"

"Maybe."

The bartender replaced Kristi's cocktail napkin and asked Marcus if he needed anything else. Without giving it any thought, Marcus ordered "what she's having."

Kristi said, "But no Herculaneum scroll can legally leave Italy if it was recently dug up. And we don't know the provenance of the scroll."

"There is that," Marcus said. "But if someone could claim they purchased it from someone else who got it a century ago, before all these heritage protection laws came into effect, it could be listed at Sotheby's, I guess. Or sold on eBay. Or maybe to the Holy Books Foundation."

"It sounds like you've been thinking about what you could do with the scroll if it turns up."

"I'm always thinking about that scroll. But not to make money from it. I want to write about it."

"You and me both."

A clatter of spoons, saucers, and cups from behind the bar chimed along with Miles. An espresso was being made, its banging and vacuuming soundscape as fundamental to Naples as the motorcycles buzzing outside.

"I finally want to write the sort of history I always wanted to write," Marcus said. "Make up for lost time. And maybe I'll get a chance with this strange old friend of Gerald's." He recounted his meeting with Sweeney, and how the piece of Marcus's scroll unrolled by Laszlo was now in the old man's possession.

Kristi shook her head. "You didn't press him for more details?" she said in a reproving tone. "You didn't connect any dots from Ballard to Cipressi to him?"

"It occurred to me, of course. Because everyone knows everyone else in this business. Still, the idea of a non-invasive way to read the scrolls is very much out there. It's the silver bullet. Every papyrologist and their kid sister is talking about it. I can't sit on my hands anymore. Something has to give."

"Hold on," Kristi said. "Maybe the reason why people care about the Caesar scroll is not what's written on it. Maybe it's the *technology* that they are after. The tech used to decipher a scroll virtually. Tech that can only be tested on a carbonized papyrus scroll, the sort of scroll that's only been found at Herculaneum. That's gotta be worth something, no?"

"Presumably," Marcus said.

"I need to speak with Cipressi," she said. "He hasn't responded to my email. I need to make it happen. If there's a tech silver bullet, he would know about it."

30

CHIAIA

Tom Sweeney cherished old stamps. He had collected them as a kid, and the most exotic specimens, in particular those from the former French colonies of Indochina — the elephants, curved roofs, and goddesses — had excited his imagination. Despite, or because of, a long career focused on codes and algorithms, he was always delighted to receive an actual letter.

Nonius carried in the daily batch of mail on a silver tray with fanciful handles. Sweeney eyed the various postmarks, his brow furrowing at one of them: an envelope from the National Prosecutor's Office of the Italian Republic. It contained a letter written in awkward English, stating that Signor T.J. Sweeney was required for an interview in connection with a case involving trafficking in antiquities. His presence without delay at the Naples state prosecutor's office was requested.

Which antiquities? His entire palazzo was filled with them. Was this because of that police officer who had visited him recently? She claimed to be there in relation to Ballard. But perhaps she was on a fishing expedition, snooping around.

For years now, Sweeney had endeavoured to avoid publicity and controversy. He subscribed to a system of thought that shunned political engagement or activism of any kind. Such efforts could only lead to an assault on *ataraxia*. He had been careful, retired for the most part, living a life of comfort and quiet.

His one exception to this reclusive ideal was the ambition to decipher a Herculaneum papyrus. The venture's commercial potential motivated him, of course. If the Herculaneum scrolls could be virtually unrolled, the same non-invasive technology could be applied to other damaged historical documents: medieval books with their cannibalized texts as bindings; soiled bamboo scrolls from China; letters from the Franklin expedition. The possibilities were vast and very lucrative.

A grand project, from his point of view, maybe the grandest, to ultimately make the world a better place. He aimed to play a lead role in deciphering ancient masterpieces, philosophical tracts to guide the future of mankind, nothing less than blueprints for *the good life* and well worth any inconveniences along the way.

Sweeney was fond of the Latin maxim *quod non est in actis non est in mundo*: if it's not documented, it does not exist. Once upon a time in Italy, maybe eighty years back, the state required a *certificato di esistenza in vita*. Breathing wasn't sufficient evidence that you were actually alive. A bona fide document was needed to prove that fact.

Not that being alive, documented or not, lasted tremendously long. He'd had a good kick at the can, but the end was clearly in sight. And end it would be, without leaving a trace. Sweeney had never fathered any children, but even if he had, their memories of him, and then those of any grandchildren, would endure less than a century after his death. Mankind so often consoled itself with puny legacies. What truly remained was hard evidence.

So much the better if, as a byproduct of his work, a great deal of wealth had accrued. Even that pedantic philosopher Philodemus, so dear to the hearts of Herculaneum scholars, wrote that the wise man desired affluence. Epicurus himself was reportedly content with very little, but nothing in his system opposed material comforts. In any case, Sweeney could use his wealth for causes far more beneficial to humanity than lining the pockets of entitled offspring. But at the moment he felt annoyingly unmoored. One risk factor had led to another; the risks seemed to be boiling over beyond his control. So be it. *Alea iacta est*: the die is cast.

31

CENTRO STORICO

"I think Epicurus lived a life of fear. He's a bad role model for you."

"How so?"

Marcus had walked Kristi to her Airbnb. And outside the dilapidated palazzo, whether due to prosecco or jet lag or the atmosphere of Naples, a goodnight hug had swerved into something more.

"He was obsessed with the possible negative repercussions of everything," Kristi said.

He voiced something that was muffled by the pillow, a sound equal parts hangover groan and hedonistic humming. In fact, he could not have been happier.

"No, really. Don't eat or drink too much because you'll pay the price tomorrow. Don't get married or have children; that's *way* too messy. Don't get involved in politics because it will lead to headaches and difficulties."

He managed to utter a croaky, "Okay. Still, I won't be drinking anymore." Marcus wasn't used to alcohol or to its morning-after effects.

At the hotel bar, her prosecco had looked so good, and she seemed to be so thoroughly enjoying it that he ordered a glass of the effervescent beverage. And then a few more.

"You remind me of your Facebook photo right now," she said.

"Is that good or bad?"

"Well, that profile pic with your long tresses does make you look cooler than you actually are in person." She ran her fingers through his hair fanned out on the big pillow.

"Grazie mille."

They were on a futon in her little studio — seventy-four euros per night, low-season rate. Morning light filtered through the threadbare curtains at a bay window. From street level came tooting horns and revving engines that somehow managed to sound soothing.

Marcus turned and caressed her neck down to her waist, a cartographer mapping out a newly discovered coastline and feeling a sea change in himself.

She steered the conversation back to philosophy. "For all his talk about living in the moment, Epicurus couldn't have been doing much of it. He was hiding from it. So many chess moves trying to anticipate the consequences of every possible action. I'm surprised he got out of bed in the morning."

Marcus said, "Maybe he didn't have a compelling reason to stay in bed." His hand gravitated to her neck and corralled her hair into a ponytail.

"It seems like you agree with him that the world's a dangerous place," she said. "Alcohol may be fun, but it will make you do and say things you may regret and then keep you up at night. Partake of the wrong food or drink and you'll kick the bucket. As to politics, you prefer playing devil's advocate. And like him you acknowledge that the gods may exist in some distant realm but don't intervene in human life."

He was very much awake at this point. "May I suggest you're being a bit harsh? If your mother expired at fifty-three, you might think twice about tempting fate. And you don't appreciate the fact that being a good sleeper is a gift from the gods. In whatever distant realm they occupy."

He was all too familiar with garden-variety insomnia. This current fatigue was of a superior quality to the versions he was used to. Being sleep-deprived for a good reason made all the difference.

"Live a little!" she said.

Marcus considered that. A line from Philodemus came to mind: mortality is necessary because, without it, life would cease to have value. The constant threat of annihilation made the need to live well that much more pronounced. That old Neapolitan proverb *campa un giorno e campalo bene*. Live for the day and live it well. In Naples, shadowed by the volcano, imperiled by so many mortal threats, people lived well.

"I'll give it some thought."

He turned over onto his back and she nestled her head on his chest, his heartbeat a comforting, steady mantra, keeping a sort of slow trip-hop time with the racket from outside. Her fingers traced circles on his stomach.

"You think too much. Like Epicurus. You think you can control everything. Sleep, cholesterol, safety, Gerald's financial investments. But you can't. You never can."

"I know. Man makes plans, Zeus laughs."

"Nice. Where's that from — Homer?"

"No, an old Yiddish proverb."

Marcus knew she was onto something. He flashed back to a time in his life when he was less self-protective, when he dared to take chances and damn the torpedoes. He had another thought and fumbled for his phone, searching for a file he'd compiled during those long, information-gathering days in the Toronto library.

"Check this out. An epigram by Philodemus."

She rolled her eyes. "Spare me."

"Listen. The scene is probably not far from here, maybe right here in the old part of Naples. Philodemus is speaking about his lover. She is, I think, playing the lyre for him.

> Xanthippe's touch on the lyre,
> and her talk, and her speaking eyes,
> and her singing, and the fire
> that is just alight,
> will burn thee, my heart,
> but from what beginning
> or when or how I know not."

"Knew I forgot to pack something," Kristi said. "My lyre."
"Hold on. Here's another one.

> I loved. Who hasn't?
> I made revels in her honour.
> Who hasn't revelled?
> But I was deranged —
> by whom? A god?
> Forget it; now grey hair
> hurries in to replace the black.
> I have reached the age of discretion.
> I played when it was time to play;
> now I turn to worthier thoughts."

A snippet of the Beck song "Paper Tiger," the new ringtone on his cell, interrupted the poetry reading.
"Saved by the bell!" she said.
"Hello? Yes, it's Marcus. Good to hear from you . . . Sure. In a few hours? Okay . . . At your place? . . . Did you find anything? . . . Okay. That's fine. See you then. Goodbye."

"Who was that?"

Marcus was already out of bed, getting into his jeans and looking for the rest of his scattered clothes.

"Sweeney. He wants to meet as soon as possible. He has news."

32

CHIAIA

Thomas Sweeney removed the scroll from its plastic container. An underwhelming object that looked to all the world like a fat sausage left for days on a barbeque. Yet in his mind's eye he could see through the contours of the papyrus; he imagined peering through its fused layers and reading what lay inside. That was what had in fact transpired after it was shipped off to the European Synchrotron Radiation Facility in Grenoble, France.

Now pure luck had placed the missing link in his hands. The unrolled papyrus segment that Marcus Sinclair had lent him was clearly part and parcel of the same scroll. The Caesar scroll. That certainly had a ring to it. And what a stunning text to have employed for his proof of concept!

Well, he deserved the luck. Earned it. *Fortune favours the bold*: he often reassured himself with that line from Virgil. Fortune also favoured the scroll, this scroll, anyway.

He thought back to some fifteen years earlier, when one particularly bold idea got off the ground. It was on a gorgeous red clay tennis court, a mile or so from the Golden Gate Bridge, Gerald Sinclair on the other side of the net. Despite Gerald's age — he was well into his seventies, getting on in tennis years — he had a rocket of a serve, flat with impressive pace, a weapon that could be relied on to keep him in most games.

Sweeney visualized his younger self: hair Björn Borg style, with a headband. He was too much the nonconformist for golf, but he hadn't learned tennis at a sufficiently young age to be very good. What he lacked in technique, though, he made up for with anaerobic skill, his dogged ability to stop and start on a dime, to run down every shot, all the while using a newfangled Yonex R-22 graphite racquet.

He was well aware that his opponent, Gerald Sinclair, always employed some sort of edge in life for every endeavour, be it gems stashed in his pants to get out of Nazi territory (a story Sweeney had been regaled with) or a business connection to an unorthodox dealer (about which Gerald was tight-lipped). In tennis, Gerald's cannon of a serve provided that edge.

The older man was up 5–4 in games, serving for the set. His first serve, delivered by a wooden Dunlop Maxply, came in low and hard but clipped the top of the net and landed out. He put even more pace into his second serve. The yellow ball landed bang on the service line of the clay court, skidding, impossible to return.

A risky move to launch a second serve with that much power. And yet, another example of audacity bringing success. Gerald appeared more than happy to win with an ace, even if hitting the line seemed less than fair to his opponent.

"I won't say you got lucky on that one," Sweeney remembered saying, seated for pints of beer. "Okay, I'll say it. You had a horseshoe up your ass."

The tennis club was decorated with old-timey rackets and framed photos of club grandees going back a century.

Gerald had replied, "You make your own luck. In tennis as in life."

"You hit the line! That's not something anyone can aim for."

The conversation was firmly lodged in Sweeney's memory.

"Let's just say I know how to avoid, but only just, crossing lines."

"Speaking of which . . ."

The men paused to swig their beers and consider their next moves. Tennis for them was transactional as much as golf was for other businessmen.

"I'm looking for a papyrus scroll," said Sweeney.

"An unusual request."

"But doable, I'm hoping?"

"I can put out feelers. Any particular kind of papyrus?"

"Not really. But we both know the only realistic source for such scrolls. Nothing from an Egyptian rubbish heap. I want it to be literary. And potentially readable. Still rolled."

"A tall order. And there is no market value for such things. Are you getting literary on me, Tom?"

"Possibly. But there's a technology angle here. Another code I want to break. You like lines. I like zeros and ones."

Gerald Sinclair said, "Careful not to let your ball spin out of control."

"No risk there. But thanks for the concern."

What Gerald said next was classic Gerald: "Keep your shoes in mind."

"My shoes?"

"ASICS. An excellent brand of footwear. You know what the brand name stands for?"

"It's Japanese, no?"

"Latin. *Anima Sana In Corpore Sano*. A sound mind in a sound body."

Thinking back to that day, despite the Italian authorities breathing down his neck, Ballard dead, and his own state of calm being perturbed, Sweeney felt certain that what comes around goes around. He'd worked like hell and was entitled to his good fortune.

33

CENTRO STORICO

It reminded Antonio Cipressi of a beautiful mosaic of marine life discovered in Pompeii. Except the sea creatures here were real, fanning their fins and stretching their tentacles inside a vast aquarium that topped the entire bar at a restaurant called Pesca.

The original mosaic in the archaeology museum was stunning. As was a copy he'd seen in the palazzo of Thomas Sweeney.

Cipressi was waiting for her at the bar when Kristi arrived, looking very much like his online photos, a man of short stature who'd presumably been fed a lot of pasta in his life, with blue-framed glasses and a trim goatee. He sprang to his feet and shook her hand with gusto.

"What are you drinking?" he asked.

"Well, lately, prosecco. Maybe a bit too much of it."

"You're in Napoli. It cannot be too much."

He ordered her a glass as Kristi scanned the underwater scene inside the aquarium-topped bar.

"Amazing," she said.

"It is special."

Kristi extracted a notepad from her bag. "So, once again, let me say that I'm sorry about what happened to Trevor Ballard," she said.

"I wish I could know what happened exactly."

"Hopefully, eventually," she said, "the police will figure it out."

The glass of prosecco arrived. Kristi took a sip and asked Cipressi about his dealings with Ballard in Naples.

"Digital unwrapping. It's not a secret. We had similar ideas. His were connected to Google's book-scanning software. My ideas are for a synchrotron. We could have worked together."

"Yes?"

"Unfortunately we never got that far."

"But someone else may have?"

"I don't think so."

A small, purple-coloured fish swam into Kristi's field of vision. Was everything in this aquarium also on the menu?

"So," she said, resuming her focus, "what do you think happened to the scroll?"

"What scroll?"

The bartender filled a small glass of fizzy water for Kristi.

"You know, the scroll that disappeared from Ballard's hotel room."

Cipressi did not know — and this startling bit of news had him coughing up wine.

As Kristi elaborated, he kept shaking his head, muttering variations on "I can't believe it" and "That's incredible."

"Didn't the police question you about Ballard?"

"Yes. But they never mentioned a papyrus!"

"And wasn't Ballard exchanging information with you? I thought you were working with him."

"He gave me no information about a scroll, so now I'm wondering who he was really working with."

Pondering that question, they drank in silence.

Kristi finally said, "Google is not some fly-by-night operation. He must have shared some detailed plans with you?"

"Didn't you know that Ballard was not working for Google anymore?" he replied.

It was her turn to register surprise.

"Yes," he continued. "Ballard had created his own company. He was working for himself. Apparently Google recently terminated his employment because of a conflict of interest. The police told me."

Kristi had taken out her notepad and was writing down this new information. It made sense that Ballard had not been employed by Google at the time he was killed. The tech giant had not responded to any of her phone calls or emails, nor had they issued a statement about the murder of one of its senior engineers. Now it added up.

"Then there was the personal stuff," Cipressi said.

"Personal stuff meaning what?"

"Ballard told me he was 'polyamorous.' We don't have this word in Italy. We have other words, older ones. It's nothing new. But he asked me where he could meet women in Naples. I told him about Jungle Bar in Alabardieri. I told you on the phone."

"Right. Is that far from here?"

"Nothing is far away in Naples."

"I wonder if anyone there might remember Ballard? Maybe he met someone there?"

"It is, how you say, a 'pick-me-up' bar."

Kristi said, "The night is young. Can we go visit it?"

34

CHIAIA

Marcus had been summoned to Sweeney's home for an update on the papyrus scroll. The update was newsworthy. Sweeney had tracked down Gerald's scroll.

"It's a perfect match with your fragment," Sweeney was saying. "My machine-learning AI software was able to interpret both papyri, examining the age, the handwriting, the ink, the whole nine yards. It's one and the same papyrus."

Sweeney explained that an unrolled scroll had been analyzed at the Grenoble Synchrotron in southeastern France. There it had been pummelled with beams for three days. So he shipped Marcus's fragment across the French border to the same facility. "The phase-contrast tomography scan had been a particle smashing success," he told Marcus.

Working with both sets of scans at his own lab in the university district, Sweeney had employed software and machine-learning that his "team" had been experimenting with for some time. It was feared that the bumpy surface of the papyrus would present an imaging problem, but no such problem cropped up. "It was like trying to flatten a potato chip," Sweeney said. "And the potato chip was well and truly flattened."

"The best part of all is the content of the scroll. It's a collection of letters to a Roman statesman by the name of Piso. He was an interesting man, and Julius Caesar's father-in-law, no less. And what we have is, in fact, a bona fide letter from Caesar. Actually the letter, at the start of the scroll, was in two pieces. The segment you brought me. And the last part, which was on the scroll itself. We're calling it the Caesar scroll."

Marcus was listening, but only half listening, wondering, *Where on Earth did he* find *Gerald's scroll? I gave it to Ballard, and Ballard had it when he was killed. Why is he not saying a word about where it came from?*

Sweeney was talking a blue streak. "I have no doubt that lost masterpieces remain buried in the Villa. And now, with the Caesar scroll deciphered and this proof-of-concept in hand, I can exert pressure on not only archaeologists but also the Italian authorities to dig them up. We have the technology to read any scroll, regardless of wear and tear. Not to mention other problematic ancient texts the world over."

He continued, "I have a basic translation ready, which I have no problem giving you. A papyrologist whom I work with is still going over the text. I need to have all the deltas and epsilons in place before we hold a news conference. The academics will no doubt have their noses out of joint. And the Officina. They're territorial as well as pedantic. I don't want any negative publicity."

Marcus was finally able to get a word in: "How did you find it? And *where* did you find it?"

Sweeney met his gaze. "I have my ear to the ground, and it turned out to be for sale. There are so few Herculaneum papyri floating around, that when one materialized, I purchased it. Legally, I might add."

"You purchased it from who?"

"An anonymous dealer. That's how this business works, Marcus. Your uncle operated in the same world."

"But the Caesar scroll is *my* scroll. I lent it to Ballard. It is rightfully mine, no matter who stole it and sold it to you!"

Sweeney paused and sipped from his silver goblet. Finally, he said, "I was not entirely forthcoming in our earlier conversation about your uncle. I indeed did quite a lot of business with Gerald. Clever man. He knew how to work the corners and employed some dubious contractors to procure the impressive treasures that found their way into his hands. Children conscripted by gangs in Egypt were lowered into illegally dug shafts, for example; I doubt he ever boasted to you about that. Or about archaeological sites pillaged, their contents sold by criminals in exchange for weapons. And believe me, you don't want to know where those weapons ended up. The list, I'm afraid, is a long one."

He went on to say that Marcus could forget about any claim that the scroll belonged to him. That ship had sailed.

And then the old man calmly gave him an ultimatum: Marcus had to let him permanently keep the papyrus segment he had loaned him, or Sweeney would go public with information that would jeopardize everything else that Marcus had inherited from his uncle.

"I'm afraid," he said, "you have no choice but to play ball with me."

A long-forgotten feeling had welled up in Marcus while Sweeney was speaking. White-hot anger. He wanted to grab the old man by his collar and demand to see the scroll, *his* scroll, immediately.

He remembered buying a bottle of water in that convenience store, hearing the shrill sirens of the ambulance heading to the hotel where — he would learn later — Ballard's lifeless body lay. And he recalled saying the six-word Hebrew phrase that Gerald had taught him. A lot of good that prayer had done!

"Oh, Marcus, why the long face? The scroll went from Gerald to a third-party dealer to me. Your uncle will still receive credit for all he's done."

Sure he would. Marcus understood that it served Sweeney well to have a convoluted chain of provenance for the papyrus, so the greedy bastard couldn't be faulted for any dodgy acquisition that might come to light. Other people had procured the scroll; he had simply worked his deciphering magic upon it. Nobody would know, or care, that he'd gotten his paws on Gerald's scroll and that Trevor Ballard had died in the process.

35

CENTRO STORICO

The Napolimage office, owned and operated by Antonio Cipressi, was a modest setup with several computers and much scanning equipment crammed into a single small room.

Cipressi had always assumed that, by this stage of his career, his office would feature bean-bag chairs, a foosball table, yoga studio, espresso bar: all the accoutrements of a Silicon Valley setup. If he was honest with himself, that was part of what attracted him to Americans like Sweeney and Ballard: their tech street cred.

But their street cred now seemed to border on illegality. If Kristi was right — and there was no reason to think otherwise — Ballard had been in possession of a papyrus scroll from Herculaneum and never so much as *mentioned* it to him. Those late nights at Ballard's hotel room, the affable American grinding his special blend of coffee beans, had just been a sideshow. Ballard had clearly been picking Cipressi's brain for info about technology that he and he alone, minus Google, minus Cipressi, intended to employ on his papyrus.

How naive Cipressi had been!

And how had Ballard managed to get hold of the papyrus in the first place? Kristi had been tight-lipped about that. But it was obvious she knew more than she was telling. And where was it now?

He had not checked in with his contact at the Grenoble synchrotron in some time. And he *had* spoken at length to Ballard about the facility. Cipressi opened his computer, a Google Pixelbook, its back festooned with stickers of circuit board components. He went straight to his Signal app and fired off a message to the man. Any developments, by any chance, with a papyrus?

It was Cipressi's experience and expertise with the synchrotron in Grenoble that was his entree with both the papyrologists and the technologists. He was a particle physicist after all, not a classics professor, not a tech entrepreneur.

Particle physics, however, did overlap with philosophy. And ever since the Herculaneum papyri entered his life, years ago now, he'd learned a bit about ancient philosophy. Epicureanism and Stoicism, in particular. From a twenty-first-century vantage point, the philosophies obviously had crude ideas about science. Yet each system of thought offered an interesting spin on physics. He was partial to the Epicureans, for whom the world was reduced to random atoms moving in a void. No overarching purpose. So too individuals: atomized, isolated, operating in an infinite space without purpose. Made scientific sense, as did the intriguing Epicurean notion of the "swerve" — when for no apparent reason atoms occasionally departed from their mechanical, predictable movements — an idea that dovetailed with quantum mechanics.

The Stoics, meanwhile, saw everything operating in cosmic harmony. The world was an immense string instrument, vibrating with unity, meaning, fate, and goodness. Yes, goodness. How could an event like the murder of Ballard be at one with a rational cosmos — ordained by nature even, as the Stoics would have believed? Where exactly was the goodness there? Yet to interpret such a tragedy as purely random, in Epicurean terms, did not sit well with Cipressi either.

He refreshed his email and saw a message had landed from his colleague at the synchrotron. As a matter of fact, beam time at the cost of twenty-five thousand euros had been granted to an Italian company scanning a carbonized papyrus scroll from Italy. Did Cipressi know anything about this? *Santo cielo!* The name of the company commissioning the scan was PurplePapyrus.

36

HERCULANEUM

Marcus walked down the main street of Ercolano, past a replica of the Drunken Satyr statue from Herculaneum, past the Herculaneum Café and the Herculaneum Hotel, to the entranceway of the ruins.

He'd visited the archaeological site during the Friends of Herculaneum conference, four months ago, and his return now produced both memory and melancholy. He remembered exploring the area with a highly enthusiastic Trevor Ballard. "It looks like some remote village in the Middle East," Ballard had said from this very same vantage point. "After being blasted into submission and left for dead."

Marcus himself felt somewhat blasted into submission. For two days, he'd been losing sleep over what to do about Sweeney's blackmail.

He snapped a picture of the ruins, which had a certain ragtag beauty, a crumbling mosaic of pillars and paving stones, palm trees, buildings without roofs, here and there covered with red barrel tiles. The modern town of Ercolano, on higher ground, teetered precariously above old

Herculaneum. A few bulldozers could have nudged the modern town over a promontory and into the graveyard of its unlucky predecessor. Small wonder that the idea of further excavations — which would be directly beneath the modern town — was controversial.

The message Marcus received from the hotel concierge gave no hint as to who he'd be meeting. The envelope held a sheet of old paper, lighter at the edges the way sunlight faded the borders of papyrus scrolls. Hand-written in neat block letters was the message:

Meet tomorrow 16h00 at the Casa del Rilievo di Telefo in the ruins of Ercolano to rescue your papyrus.

He trudged down the footpath, paid the entrance fee, passed through a turnstile, and descended to the dusty ruins. The massive rock wall to his back was a graphic reminder of how the site had been excavated a hundred feet down from rock the consistency of cement.

Many of the homes were reduced to rubble or roofed with sheet metal, like a shantytown emptied of its residents. Tourists were similarly AWOL at the moment; there appeared to be no one milling about so late in the day. What a difference from overrun Pompeii, Herculaneum's more popular sister city, a site that drew legions of tourists.

Marcus wished he was back at the ersatz Herculaneum of the Getty Villa. There: ocean air, burbling fountains, fragrant herb gardens, and reflecting pools. Here: rubble and a large hole in the ground.

He passed the boatsheds, a dozen barrel-vaulted chambers that once formed a terrace above the beach. It was here that more than three hundred people fled the volcano, desperate to be rescued via the sea. They never made it. The tumbling clouds of superheated ash brought instant death. *We all live in a city without walls.*

He peered into one vault at the grisly skeletons awaiting digital conveyance by tourists to Facebook and Instagram. Fakes. The real skeletons were stored elsewhere for preservation and testing. Height, teeth, bone structure, evidence of disease — the doomed citizens of Herculaneum had become lab rats for future scientists.

Marcus walked along the fat cobblestones, past the statue of another Marcus, this one Marcus Nonius Balbus, once upon a time the town's major benefactor, his right arm in *Hail Caesar* mode but missing its hand. He had read somewhere that Balbus died a natural death, long before Vesuvius unloaded thermal energy equivalent to a couple of thousand Hiroshimas.

Following the site map, he progressed along Cardo V street, passing the remains of a tavern and turning right at what the map indicated was the "House of Telephus Relief." Its atrium was decorated with hanging oscilla, pie-sized marble discs carved with scenes of revelry. Three columns were coloured with what looked like an original Pompeian red, set against burgundy and burnt-orange walls. The scene could have passed for a Cecil B. DeMille film set.

A dog howled in the distance and was answered by a rooster. Marcus stepped into a hallway and beneath an archway into a small chamber.

Cigarette smoke.

He followed the nicotine trail into another room where a bearded man was sitting on the stump of a pillar, legs crossed, smoking non-chalantly as if he were in his own living room.

"*Ciao*, Marcus."

There was something oddly familiar about the man, who wore a navy button-down shirt, dark dress pants, and gleaming oxblood leather shoes. A sports jacket was draped over one leg.

"And who are you?"

"Call me Gramsci," he said. "I knew your uncle quite well."

"How do you know about me? How do you know about the papyrus?"

Gramsci exhaled smoke. "It is my business."

"Your business being?"

"Let's say, the unorthodox sale of antiquities."

Marcus felt depleted by fatigue, thirst, the stress of going out to the ruins without knowing why.

"Papyri from Ercolano do not come to the market very often," the bearded man continued. "When they do, I learn about it. When, for example, a dealer from America comes to Napoli looking for a papyrus, I learn about it. And when his nephew comes back to Napoli with the same papyrus many years later, I learn about it also."

It now dawned on Marcus why Gramsci's name rang a bell. He'd seen it in Gerald's Rolodex.

"When a man from Google who has the same papyrus is killed, I learn about it. Too late, maybe. And when I learn that an American, Signor Sweeney, has taken Geraldo's papyrus, I learn about it. None of this is good for my business."

A young Italian man with a badge appeared and shouted something about "*fumare*." A discussion ensued that Marcus half understood to be about whether smoking was permitted on the site. The man with the badge seemed mollified and left.

"You know, our government has a very small budget for this place. Only a few officials can be hired to supervise the homes here. That man is one of them." He let the cigarette drop to the ground and ground it under his right shoe. "So, your papyrus. I have sweet memories of this papyrus. I liked your uncle. I don't like everyone I have business with. But I liked Geraldo. Very much. And he would not be happy that this man has stolen his papyrus."

"How do you know about what Sweeney did?"

"There is a tradition that anyone who steals something from Herculaneum gets a *malediction*. A curse, no? Not so long ago, a *maschera*, a mask from the theatre, was taken from the Casa Neptune. The malediction must have been functional because, months later, the thief mailed it back via the postal service."

"Wouldn't that apply to your activities?"

Gramsci lit another cigarette and made a sucking sound, frowned, and exhaled, his face wreathed in smoke. "This is about Signor Sweeney. My methods are connected to a tradition, a business that has gone on for a very long time. He is not from here and deserves what malediction gives him.

"But we don't have time for a long conversation. That guard will come back soon. Okay, there are two things I will tell you. One is the alarm code to Sweeney's home." Reaching inside his jacket, Gramsci pulled out a package and handed it to Marcus.

"What is this?"

Gramsci stamped his cigarette out on the ground. "This will help you get the papyrus. There is one bullet in it. It might not even function, an old Russian thing that was used in Hungary many years ago. It doesn't matter. It is a menace. It is protection. You will not fire it. But take it with you.

"The alarm code is also inside. I expect nothing. Do as you want to. I can only tell you that Sweeney plans never to give Gerald's papyrus to you."

Gramsci carefully rolled up his shirt sleeves, and Marcus noticed on his forearm a tattoo of a rose accompanied by a few letters. The Italian got to his feet, briskly slapped some dust off his pants and said, "Please do not follow me. We must leave separately. *Buona fortuna*, Marcus."

37

METRO TOLEDO

Cipressi gathered up his notes and placed them in a plastic box already filled to the brim. There were many such boxes stacked on the shelves of his office, all containing his true love, calculations about quantum gravity. But uppermost in his mind was something with the ridiculous name of PurplePapyrus.

Thomas Sweeney's company of that name had shipped a scroll to the Grenoble synchrotron. Without Cipressi's knowledge. Of course, Sweeney — like Ballard — had quizzed Cipressi ad nauseam about how to approach them, what settings to request, the rotation algorithms required, and for how long the scroll should be X-rayed, based on Cipressi's in-depth research into the problem. Cipressi had no idea whether the experiment would work. But that was beside the point. Both men had — independently — been slyly ripping off his ideas while giving him nothing in return, even though he was led to believe that he would be part of some well-financed future project.

He walked over to a bookshelf that held an Einstein doll, a gift from his young daughter. A disturbing thought sprang to mind. He emailed his contact at the synchrotron. Had Trevor Ballard or Google been involved in this PurplePapyrus scan? He made a typing error, and *scan* ended up as *scam*, which he quickly corrected. The reply came back quickly: *Non.*

Another disturbing thought pulsated. Had Sweeney killed Ballard to muscle in on the technology they'd all been experimenting with? Was Cipressi's own life in danger? There wasn't much to go on, but enough to notify police, which he'd do first thing tomorrow. Let the cops join the dots. He had nothing to hide.

He was holding a squeeze ball to relieve tension. It was designed like a spherical cow, that well-known science joke, a gift from physics students he'd taught. What would those innocent minds think about his current conundrum? First and foremost, he blamed himself. He'd been seduced by the prospect of tech breakthroughs involving Google or Sweeney, but a breakthrough that leaned heavily on his own calculations and knowledge of synchrotron physics. He wanted to jump-start a career that was stuck in neutral, his cash-strapped finances inadequate for two young children, as well as alimony payments.

This was his week without the kids, so he worked late into the night. It was well past midnight when he finally left the office and took his usual route down Via Toledo to the subway station. The psychedelic artwork of the Toledo station suggested the interior of a chemical nucleus. Cipressi rode the escalator down to the platform.

The platform was deserted. Cipressi considered how he'd set out on a conventional course in life with no daring intervals until a vacation in Capri one summer when he happened to be staying at a hotel where a convention of classicists was meeting. One discussion at the hotel bar led to others. He kept in touch. Kept scribbling his ideas about synchrotron hardware and quantum imaging. The virtual unwrapping breakthrough finally seemed doable.

He checked his Signal account. Nothing more from Grenoble. But another email from the journalist, Kristi Grainger. She should be informed about all he knew and suspected about Sweeney. Despite the late hour, he fired off an email from his phone.

38

MATERDEI

Among the joys of driving her Vespa was the fact that Zuccarello could not be recognized in the black helmet and protective goggles. Just another Neapolitan commuter on two wheels, a soloist in a city orchestra tuning up, roaring, shifting, and screeching. She wasn't paranoid, but being chief of homicide in Naples came with a bull's eye on your back. Zipping through traffic — aerodynamic and anonymous — was a pleasurable disguise.

On this morning rush hour, she weaved her way to a pole position at a stoplight. To her right, the massive archaeology museum glowed in the rising sun; the metal on motorcycles glistened. Let her friends drone on about morning meditation; this was her time to be at one with the universe. The light turned green, and Zuccarello motored up the steep stretch of Via Toledo, entering the Materdei district.

Giuseppe had already visited Festa pizzeria and had come up empty-handed, except for the margherita pizza he managed to receive on the house. But was there really no CCTV footage in the restaurant? No security cameras anywhere outside it? And she wanted to go through the receipts for the afternoon Ballard had lunch there just hours before he became a homicide victim. Escaping from her dreary office was further incentive for Zuccarello, as was the opportunity to grab a coffee that didn't pop out of a vending machine.

Another traffic light had her stopped beside a greengrocer with produce spilling over onto the sidewalk. Dwarfing the lemons and apples were huge watermelons arrayed on a metal rack like some avant-garde art installation. One watermelon was sliced in half to flaunt its bright red flesh, which made her think of the blood in Ballard's hotel sink.

The traffic light turned green, and a few minutes later, she parked the Vespa and walked along the pitted cobblestones to Festa. Indeed, no security cameras lurked outside. The restaurant was closed, but peering through the glass door plastered with menus she could see someone inside. A knock on the door resulted in a middle-aged woman tapping her wristwatch. Closed, yes, obviously. Zuccarello made a more metallic noise, the sound of her police badge clanking against the door.

The woman inside padded over to the door, turned several locks, and with some effort, slid open a deadbolt. The door inched open.

"We're closed," she said.

"I'm not here for pizza."

Fifteen minutes later, Zuccarello was sifting through a stack of receipts in search of Ballard's bill. Credit card records had already pinpointed to police the time of the former Google engineer's last transaction. That made her search relatively easy.

The woman who'd unlocked Festa's door was the restaurant's bookkeeper. Wearing wire-rimmed glasses and turquoise earrings, she appeared frazzled by the police visit and made a phone call, speaking in hushed tones to what must have been her boss.

Zuccarello had to admit that Festa's records were well-maintained and above board. It was a big restaurant with multiple dining rooms, a labyrinthine setup with a brisk turnover, according to its records. The receipts for the afternoon in question, August 2, were arranged in several piles bound by elastic bands. The large number of "*conti*" suggested the restaurant was not doing cash sales.

She was seated at the reception desk with its gleaming white countertop. On the counter was an old-fashioned bell and a Coca-Cola can that served as a tip jar, a hand-scrawled *GRAZIE* sign taped to it. The main decor was a wall-sized bulletin board filled with snapshots of notable customers posing at the pizzeria. If only Ballard had been famous enough to pose for a pic.

From just outside, the sound of a motorcycle engine revved, sputtered, and shut down. "The manager is here," said the bookkeeper.

Zuccarello was preoccupied; she'd found the receipt she'd been searching for. The time code of 14:36 corresponded, and the tab — sixty-four euros — approximately fit the credit card charge converted to dollars.

The pizzeria's door swung open and a thirty-something man in a white windbreaker with black racing stripes made a noisy entrance. "I'm the manager," he said. "What's going on? We pay our taxes. Unlike everyone else."

Zuccarello placed one hand on the pile to keep her place. "This is not about taxes."

"So? What's this about?"

"A homicide investigation."

The manager approached the reception counter and said, "The Google guy? A cop was already here. We told him everything we know."

"Except this," Zuccarello said. She tapped an index finger twice on the bill she'd been examining.

"Meaning what?"

"This is evidence," Zuccarello said.

The manager picked up the bill and took a few seconds to read it. "The Google guy's *conto*?"

Zuccarello replied that it was — at least, she thought it was.

The restaurant manager picked up another piece of paper, read it, and said, "Maybe. The waiter's order says it was an American."

"What do you mean? Where?"

He explained that the *conto* was paired with the waiter's order notes, a system Festa used to make sure all orders were getting properly charged. In this case, the order showed "two pizzas, a Siciliana for the American and Quattro Formaggi for the Italian. Two draft beers, Don Antonio Helles, and for desert, a fried angioletti with Nutella and pistachio cream, and two espressos. Table service, four euros."

Zuccarello's eyes lit up: "The Italian?"

"Yes, the Italian ordered the Quattro Formaggi, the American got the Siciliana pizza. The waiter's order notes are clear. It's all here."

"Ballard ate here with an Italian."

39

CHIAIA

The "swerve" is rooted in the Epicurean view of natural science. Elementary particles — *atomos* they called them — move randomly, sometimes colliding by chance with other particles. Human decision-making, it was believed, echoed the principles of Epicurean physics; there were swerves in people's minds too. This built-in unpredictability saved humans from the decrees of fate.

Say, for example, Philodemus is going about his day as usual, walking to the market in Neapolis with his lover, Xanthippe. When they arrive at the olive oil emporium, a drunken lout tries to move in on Xanthippe. She ignores him, and the drunkard makes a lewd gesture. Suddenly, Philodemus grabs a small amphora from a nearby stand and smashes it over the head of the man. He did not have to do this. It resulted from a swerve in his decision-making process.

In physical terms, not all atomic motions are causally determined. In human terms, we have the power of what the Romans called *libera voluntas*: free will. It is erratic, random, highly subjective.

Marcus had gleaned all this theory from ancient philosophy, which thanks to Gerald, he'd immersed himself in. Marcus had the peculiar sensation that something novel deep inside him was activated. It was a bolstered sense of power, as if his perennial drifting had come to an abrupt stop. It was part anger. He'd tried to process the rage that was welling up inside, to absorb it and rationalize it away as best he could. But it was no use. His emotional attachment to the scroll had only deepened in the hours since Sweeney said it would never be his again.

Once he stopped to think about it, why should he worry about Sweeney's blackmail? Could the allegations even be believed? If so, he might lose a few valuable items here and there, like the amphora. But there was no way his uncle's entire *estate* was going to be seized because some embittered associate alleged dubious trading. Besides, any such allegation would likely implicate Sweeney himself in some way.

Kristi's text, sent just a few hours earlier, had tipped the scales for Marcus. She'd received a midnight email from Cipressi with news the physicist was anxious to convey. Cipressi apparently learned that the Caesar scroll had been in Sweeney's hands months ago. Months ago! Long before Marcus had asked him to track it down.

A keypad was positioned beside the snake door knocker. Gaining entry to Sweeney's home proved a cinch. Gramsci was correct about the alarm code; the lock yielded without a murmur of protest.

It was 4:09 a.m. The portrait busts in the hallway glowed eerily in the light of Marcus's headlamp, normally used for reading in bed. He passed through the atrium, treading catlike along the mosaic tile floor between the wall and the pool.

The alarm was easily enough disabled. Sweeney would be sleeping in one of the bedrooms upstairs, knocked out on the sleeping pill he'd mentioned he was in the habit of taking. But who knew what other security precautions he might take?

The atrium led to what was apparently called the *tablinum*, the room where they'd last met, where Marcus last saw the papyrus in a vitrine displaying various artifacts. The mosaic tile floor allowed him to make his way silently. The light from the headlamp was minimal but focused, ideal for the task at hand.

The world pulverizes us, Marcus thought. A strange thought. He'd never focused before on the extent to which the world had indeed pulverized him; but it had, and at the moment he felt keenly aware of the fact. And equally aware that such a state of affairs required striking out with an audacious manoeuvre. He would retrieve the papyrus. It rightfully belonged to him. Let Sweeney reap the fruits of his "phase-contrast tomography" breakthrough on some other scrap of history. This one meant something to him.

The glass vitrine displayed oil lamps, a silver cup, a bronze statuette, and some glass and metal works that Sweeney had boasted about. The thin beam from his headlamp shifted from one object to the next. The scroll had occupied pride of place there during their earlier meeting. It had looked like a misshapen lump of coal next to more elegant artifacts.

But the scroll was gone. He remembered precisely where the papyrus had been placed in the vitrine, a spot that was now empty. He wheeled around to search elsewhere. His headlamp lit on an unexpected figure.

"I told you I was an insomniac."

Sweeney was sitting on one of those long Roman couches. *Yes*, thought Marcus, struggling to contain his panic, *an insomniac reliant on sleeping pills. So much for that calculus.*

"There are some nights when I just don't sleep. Don't even make the attempt. Taking pills night after night scrambles this old brain. So occasionally I soldier on without meds. Coincidence then, or maybe fate, that tonight is one of those nights. A *nuit blanche*, as they say."

Sweeney sipped from a goblet. "But I assumed you're a good sleeper, Marcus. Having an off-night, are we? Maybe there's something in the air. I've often wondered how it is that friends often experience sleeplessness on the very same nights."

"I'm here for Gerald's scroll."

"Gerald's scroll? The ownership question can be argued from several different angles. Let's not debate the issue at this late hour."

The old man looked like a cartoon version of himself, in powder-blue pajamas and matching slippers.

Marcus said, "Where is it?"

"I'm not inclined to answer that question. I explained how going public about Gerald's methods would not be in your best interest. Why don't you call it a night, and we'll pass this off as a curious case of sleepwalking."

"You've done your tinkering on my scroll. Stealing it wasn't part of any deal that I made. Or that Trevor Ballard made. I'm not leaving without it."

His hand felt for the carpenter's belt Marcus had purchased at an Italian hardware store. He'd been nervous in the cab that the heavy metal thing in the belt would go off. Walked extra cautiously as a result. Now, as if in a dream or a trance, he swerved once more and carefully unholstered his weapon.

The Tokarev TT33, emblazoned with a five-pointed star on the handle, was once upon a time used by the Soviet Red Army. Gramsci had provided a curious degree of detail about the gun in a note taped to the weapon. It had been acquired on the black market in Budapest in 1956. It spent the next generation hidden in an attic before ending up with the Italian Red Brigades. The pistol had supposedly not been fired since Budapest. A bizarre amount of provenance for an item that was hardly a collectible antiquity.

It was loaded with a very old cartridge. If the weapon had survived as well as Gerald's scroll had, it could be relied on. But Marcus had no plans to find out. Banking on the intimidation factor, he pointed the gun at Sweeney.

The old man looked up the barrel of the gun but remained calm. "The thing about building an ancient home like this," Sweeney said, "is that you can never entirely turn back the clock."

"Spare me your rhetoric."

"This rhetoric you'll want to hear, Sinclair the Younger. I've built a home that is a bona fide first-century BC replica, though it contains, of course, many conveniences of our age. Flush toilets, dishwasher, an alarm system . . . I won't say the alarm system is foolproof, given your presence here. But it does include, inconveniently for your current adventure, security cameras."

The gun's handle was embossed with tiny grooves that provided a grippy surface. Its metal felt pleasantly cool and weighty in a hand used to pen and paper.

Sweeney took another sip from his goblet. "If you look over my right shoulder, you will notice on the wall a faithful copy of that exquisite mosaic of marine life in the Bay of Naples, discovered in a Pompeian home. You might consider it out of place. It should rightly be in the *cubiculum*. But I am not dogmatic about decor. And if you look at the mosaic, you will see a lobster, eels, squid, various fish, and, dead centre, an octopus.

"And in the octopus's left eye is a security camera which is, in fact, pointing straight at you."

Marcus kept his pistol hand steady and shifted his gaze to the mosaic in question. Nice craftsmanship. He'd seen the original in the archaeology museum. At that instant he felt an explosive pain at the back of his head and the room blurred, admitting tiny pinpricks of light before turning black, as pitch-black as the charred papyrus scroll.

40

MOUNT VESUVIUS

Kristi had no difficulty keeping up with Lorenzo while hiking the steep slope of Vesuvius. Between SoulCycle spin classes and hot yoga, she was in good shape. She clambered ahead with a small knapsack on her back, wearing form-fitting sweatpants and turquoise running shoes.

Despite the unseasonably cold weather and the possibility of rain, they agreed to take a serious hike, not the touristy stroll after a bus ride that conveyed visitors most of the way up. She was keen to see Vesuvius, though she mainly wanted another opportunity to pick Lorenzo and Christoph's brains for information. Christoph, however, declined at the last minute to join them, citing a minor accident on his bicycle.

"He would have been safer on a motorcycle," Lorenzo had said. Kristi ignored that critique and wanted to know whether Christoph was injured in any serious way. Apparently he wasn't.

Her thoughts now turned elsewhere: Cipressi had emailed her

sometime around midnight and she in turn texted Marcus with bombshell news: Sweeney had come into possession of "Ballard's scroll" *two months* ago. So the Caesar scroll presumably went from Marcus to Ballard to Sweeney. She had plans to meet Cipressi that evening and learn more.

She'd tried Marcus a few hours ago, but his cell was turned off. She decided to stick with her plans for the hike, hoping to fill in more blanks of a puzzle that was slowly taking shape.

"I love this volcano," Lorenzo was now saying.

"Love? I thought most sensible people feared the thing."

"If not for Vesuvius, we would not have the papyri. It has given so much."

Kristi kept up her pace, staying on the topic of the scrolls and the new, promising technologies that were out there.

"Big Tech," said Lorenzo. "You know what happens when Google and Facebook and Amazon control everything. Like what you said happened to your newspaper."

"Yes, but newspapers don't need to be deciphered by high tech. Carbonized papyrus scrolls do."

Soon they approached the eight-hundred-metre mark, where the path forked. To the left, it led to the narrow valley known as the Atrio del Cavallo. Lorenzo took the trail to the right, winding upwards to the steep sides of the volcano.

Lorenzo said, "I'm doing quite fine with old technology."

Higher up, fumaroles, wisps of smoke, were issuing from the upper shelves of the crater. "Sure," Kristi said. "But the more technology the better, no? How else is anyone ever going to read the stuff?"

The landscape, which had been lush and green, laced with old lava flows shaped like the petrified claws of a giant predator, gave way to a bone-dry, red-tinged soil, a Martian ecosystem.

Lorenzo said, "The methods we use work very well. Professor Brill has gone thirty years with only a microscope, and he's brought two books to life! Professor Jensen spent twenty years on one book. A genius book. Professor Auger didn't need Google to make his career. And one day, I will make my edition. I just need a tenure-track position. Or another post-doc fellowship. I need time."

They briefly stopped to swig some water and looked ahead: the huge grey crater of the volcano rose up like a UFO forced to make an emergency landing.

"Okay," Kristi said, "but why take twenty years to edit a text if you can do it in months?"

"That is how scholarship works. You know, we have waited two thousand years for the scrolls. They don't need to be read in one week. And if suddenly one thousand papyri were unrolled there would be nobody to interpret them so fast. It is not like spaghetti in water. It *has* to take a long time."

They made it to La Capannuccia, the small snack bar at the end of a path normally filled with tourists. But the weather was bleak with a light drizzle of rain, the snack bar boarded up, the famous view nonexistent, and nary a tourist in sight. An English sign warned, *AUTHORIZED ONLY — all-terrain vehicles permitted and nothing else beyond this point.* Yet there was no official on duty, it seemed, and they could walk around to the far end of the vast crater unimpeded if they pushed ahead. So Kristi followed Lorenzo, who picked up his pace while words streamed out of him.

"If Google does what it wants," he said, "they would also control all the papyri they open virtually. It would be a *virtual* dictatorship. That's what it would be. Big Data doesn't understand our world. We are standing on the shoulders of great scholars who came before us. We're not standing on algorithms. We're not standing on clicks. Silicon Valley engineers like Trevor don't understand that."

Trevor? A red warning light lit up, and Kristi's pace slowed. Lorenzo had said he'd only met Ballard once and certainly hadn't referred to him as Trevor before. She felt like a depth charge had gone off in her body.

41

CENTRO STORICO

Marcus had regained consciousness only to find himself tied to a hard-backed chair in the *tablinum*, where he'd confronted Sweeney with disastrous results. His ears were ringing, and the back of his head felt like it was on fire. For the next several hours he was alone in the dark room, worrying about what the old man could possibly have in mind for him. If Sweeney had murdered Ballard, would he think twice about eliminating an armed intruder determined to get the papyrus back? And what about that discussion he'd overheard about Lorenzo?

Marcus never intended to fire the gun; he didn't even think that old geezer of a weapon could discharge a bullet. Now he had neither the papyrus nor the piece of it unrolled by Laszlo. And his life was in danger. *Why did I embark on such a reckless adventure? Why?*

He panicked when Nonius, holding the Tokarev gun, entered the room and untied him, then briskly steered Marcus across the tile floor like a nightclub bouncer past closing time. "Just close your mouth,"

Nonius said, giving him back the unloaded gun in a plastic bag. Dazed, Marcus weakly asked again for his papyrus.

"Get outta here."

Marcus hadn't heard Nonius speak English during his previous visits to the palazzo. But when he was slowly coming to after being bashed on the head by the man, he overheard an astonishing bit of conversation in his native tongue. Sweeney instructed Nonius to get in touch with "Lorenzo." And Nonius had replied, "Should I go to the Officina or his home?"

"Stay away from the Officina," Sweeney replied. Or something to that effect.

He then heard something else. Nonius asked Sweeney what to do about "him," presumably Marcus. Sweeney mused about his options, saying that he was tempted to call the police to report the intruder but didn't want the cops snooping around his home. "Let me think about it," he said. "Meanwhile, you speak to Lorenzo."

Marcus wondered whether he had dreamed the dialogue, given how much his head hurt. Yet there was no reason for him to have hallucinated the conversation.

Outside Sweeney's palazzo, he tried Kristi's cell, but it went straight to voicemail. *Hi! Leave a message and I will get back to you as soon as the spirit moves me.* Then he took a taxi to her Airbnb. All the apartment buzzers unanswered, he remembered that she had plans to hike Vesuvius with Lorenzo and Christoph.

Lorenzo!

Marcus tried her phone again in vain. He exited the hotel and took a taxi to the only authority he could think of. At the security entrance, Zuccarello listened with a look of growing concern as Marcus handed over Gramsci's gun in a bag and blurted out his story, talking non-stop in the elevator, feeling entirely lucid and aware how bizarre his story was. Once inside the office, the one with the snow globes,

Zuccarello placed the gun in a cardboard box, then guided Marcus into a windowless interrogation room.

As he recounted his escapade gone wrong, they were interrupted several times by plainclothes officers with pistols tucked under their shirts. Commands were barked; cops in a variety of eye-catching uniforms were coming and going. Zuccarello ordered a squad car to Sweeney's address.

Marcus repeated his main reason for being there: Lorenzo. Sweeney must have obtained his scroll from Lorenzo, meaning Lorenzo stole it from Ballard. Killed Ballard. Or might it have been Nonius?

"Lorenzo Clemente," Zuccarello said.

"One of the papyrus scholars," Marcus said. "I saw him at the conference. My journalist friend Kristi is hiking Vesuvius right now with him and Christoph, another academic. They were in a group that I climbed the volcano with. Maybe they're in this together. You can find them."

Also seated at the long table was Zuccarello's junior, the bored detective. Giuseppe, who no longer seemed bored, started to speak in English before switching to Italian, something about Lorenzo having lunch with Ballard at Festa on the day he died.

Zuccarello shot Giuseppe a look of disapproval.

Were the two young papyrologists behind Ballard's murder? Had their motivation been the theft of the Caesar scroll? And what were they doing with Kristi? "You have to find them," Marcus repeated. "Kristi may be in danger."

Two mornings ago felt like ages ago. Entwined, every movement, every touch, effortless pleasure. A feeling that lingered in her affectionate doodle on a cocktail napkin, embellished with a smiley face and a silhouette of the volcano: a jaunty sketch that now took on a sinister quality.

"Worry about your own situation, which is problematic," Zuccarello said. Still, Marcus glimpsed alarm in the homicide cop's eyes, her coolness left behind in the office with snow globes. "We will find them," she said.

"But you're saying Lorenzo was with Ballard the afternoon he was killed," Marcus said. "And Sweeney told his butler, his assistant, whatever the hell he is, that guy Nonius, to go see Lorenzo. I heard him. I'm worried. I'm begging you," Marcus paused, checking his phone to see whether Kristi had replied to multiple texts, "can you just locate Kristi? Kristi Grainger. You can question Lorenzo at the same time and Christoph, his German friend."

As Zuccarello paced the room and talked on the phone in rapid Italian, Marcus could half make out what she was saying. She contacted the police station at Vesuvius and ordered officers to be sent to the hiking trails. On other calls, she used the word *Officina* and the names *Lorenzo Clemente*, *Christoph Hirshleifer*, and *Kristi Grainger*.

"The weather is bad," she said. "That means small numbers of tourists will be on the volcano. Maybe none. Anyone there will be easy to find."

Marcus saw the sparsity of tourists in a more worrisome light: that anyone up there would be dangerously isolated. The room had slowly been filled with various police officers: civil guards, some rough-looking cops, Carabinieri Guardia Mobile, dressed entirely in black. A Polizia Municipale officer in navy blue, multi-pocketed cargo pants, and a bright white holster approached him. Handcuffs were produced.

"I have no choice," Zuccarello said. "You'll have to be processed for breaking and entering and for unlawful possession of a firearm. And maybe more."

42

MOUNT VESUVIUS

Kristi noticed red splotches on a jagged rock and imagined Lorenzo racing down the trail, his eyes nervously scanning the terrain, his mind racing, *her blood on his hands.* That was absurd — *or was it?* She shook the fear from her head and summoned a calming phrase: *Let me be at peace.* But his mention of "Trevor" was kicking up a storm of questions.

"So many papyri were destroyed in the old days," he was saying. "Just breaking the papyrus open and destroying it to get a small treasure for the king. Today we're more intelligent. Even if they make this virtual decipherment work, papyrologists will have to edit the text. But someone has to pay the papyrologist. We can't work for nothing."

Kristi said, "Nobody is expecting the scholars to work for free. And you'll get a tenure-track academic position one day, right? That's not nothing."

"It's almost nothing," he said, picking up his pace for the final stretch to the crater. "And it's in the future if it happens. Everyone else working on the papyri is getting rich. Have you seen all the American tech people in Napoli? They're not here for the pizza. They see gold in what's happening."

"What's happening? What do you mean?"

"I told you. Virtual decipherment."

Another alarm bell clanged in her head. Neither he nor Christoph had made much of "virtual decipherment" beyond it being a pipe dream.

Lorenzo stopped at a rock sculpture that from one angle resembled those monumental statues from Easter Island. "Lava," he said and took a step closer to Kristi. Was he moving in for a kiss? She knew that move all too well. If that's what was happening, he was anything but smooth. He no longer seemed that suave, relaxed Italian leaning back in his chair in the Piazza Bellini, fielding her questions with witty remarks while dragging on a joint. Something was off-kilter. Was she projecting danger based on his "Trevor" slip? Maybe it wasn't even a slip; maybe she was wrong — maybe he'd in fact previously referred to Ballard by his first name. *But no. Trust your instincts.* He placed his hand on her shoulder, and her defenses stiffened; she recoiled, reaching into her knapsack to do something, and retrieved her water bottle. She took a swig, resumed walking, and produced a half smile. Was he trying to seduce her — or something worse?

"And a tenure-track position," he said. "You know how hard that is to get? In Italy? For ancient Roman studies? You know what teaching assistants get for pay?"

The weather was drizzly and cold, with smoke and gas from the volcano further obscuring the dim light. They had passed only two hikers and one group of tourists descending the mountain. No surprise there were zero bars of signal on her phone. She was grateful for that middle-of-the-night email she'd sent Marcus, relaying Cipressi's info and keeping Marcus posted about her plans. The thing with Marcus, whatever it was, had come out of thin air, but she was glad for it. The email would be her SOS if one was required.

"How much *does* a teaching assistant make?" Kristi said, trying to normalize a conversation that kept veering into red zones.

"Not enough. The professors get everything. We are their slaves."

They passed scrubland studded with rocks, crimson flowers, and sweet-smelling broom. Dark brown scars — old lava, presumably — laced the hillside. The overcast sky spun; the ropey lava outcroppings seemed to be crawling in slow motion up the slope of the mountain. And suddenly they were on the moon, or that desolate part of the moon where a meteor had crashed, leaving a massive abyss. They'd made it to the Vesuvian crater, shrouded in dark clouds and steam.

Lorenzo jaunted ahead. She was following him warily — where else could she go? — as he walked slowly beside the rim of the crater. He kicked a lapilli stone soccer-ball-style. He half stumbled and kicked another stone into the gaping mouth of the volcano.

She rewound her mind again back to the piazza, where Lorenzo had all but denied he'd known Ballard, beyond a brief exchange while hiking Vesuvius. But Trevor Ballard wasn't killed on the mountain. She glanced at her cell again: no signal. The volcano was a dead zone if ever there was one. She placed her phone back in the knapsack and peeked into the crater, not wanting to get very close at this point, in fact wishing she was anywhere but there. Wisps of steam drifted up from the desolate grey nothingness.

Kristi imagined the cone from above: an ominous maw, a grim sinkhole leading to the magma-filled chamber deep within the volcano.

Lorenzo kicked another pebble. He seemed to be glaring at her. "The *gran cono*," he said, dangling one hiking shoe over the cone. Everything was covered in grey sand and ash. "It is like five hundred degrees Celsius in there. The Inferno for Dante."

Focus on the breath. Inhale, lengthen the exhales. In, out.

"You know," he said, "tourists only talk about 79 AD, but there were many other eruptions. In 1631, it killed six thousand people. They thought it was the punishment of God. People of Napoli ran to the streets and confessed their sins!"

She didn't like that factoid any more than the other ones he was bringing up. "Maybe we shouldn't test our luck by staying up here too long," she said.

"There have been like five hundred eruptions since 1631. We can never know."

Lorenzo seemed pent-up, invigorated somehow by being at the summit.

She took a deep breath. "Shall we head back? Looks like rain may finally be coming."

"No worry," he said. "It can be like this way, the weather, for days. We can enjoy the volcano better. No tourists with their guides and cameras and selfies. It's other times a circus up here."

"That reminds me," she said. "I'd like to take some pictures." She fished her phone out of her knapsack. Silence filled the air for longer than felt normal. Nothing felt normal since he'd blurted out Ballard's first name.

"The sky is terrible for photos," he said. "Look, it's all grey."

She'd turned her back to him, checking the camera settings on her phone. If her worst fears came to pass, photos synched to the Cloud might help provide a record. Marcus was always taking photos in Naples, trying to get her in the frame. What was Marcus doing now? She regretted telling him that she needed one night alone — last night — to catch up on her sleep deficit. He was an awful sleeper, restless, noisy, fidgeting. But another night spent together and he would have grilled her about the plans for Vesuvius. He might even be here with her now.

Aiming her phone at Lorenzo right off the bat felt provocative, so she pointed it toward the murky Gulf of Naples. *Snap.* A blotched-out expanse of milky grey; no gorgeous view of Capri or Ischia. *Snap.*

She shifted the camera to the path they'd followed, flanked by rope handrails. *Snap.* She'd wheel around and get a shot of him . . . but what was that? Some movement in the far distance. A person? A mirage? She zoomed in: two figures briskly ascending the rocky trail in navy blue uniforms and matching caps.

43

OFFICINA

Professor David Brill was used to holding scraps of papyrus in the air, shifting them here and there to allow the light to glance off different angles. It was like trying to read the numbers on a credit card in a dimly lit room. This was different. He had the text right smack in front of him but no actual papyrus. No black powder flaking off the material. No bumps and buckles and crevices. He never thought he'd see the day a carbonized papyrus scroll was unwrapped virtually. But here it was, and here he was.

He did not even have to be in the Officina; he could just as well have been sitting in a Neapolitan café or back home in Oxford. And yet this was where his mind worked best with a papyrus, virtual or actual. The small bust of Epicurus, the fiercely proud sunshine of Napoli streaming through the skylight, the binocular microscopes and framed posters for lectures and conferences. It was the complete experience — including the occasional melody wafting in from the opera house next door — that sharpened his focus.

The plaque on the wall facing him proclaimed that all scholars stood on the shoulders of previous generations of scholars. Yes, but today he was leaning on technology experts, not papyrologists. In fact, the actual scroll was not even in the Officina. The so-called Caesar scroll was in the safekeeping of a Carabinieri evidence vault.

It was in this very spot, moreover, that Brill had first had a glimmer of the "virtual unrolling" potential from Ballard, the poor soul. So there was something fated, something tragic, in the air here. The ancient Greeks were fond of such thoughts about fate. He was agnostic on the subject. But all the same . . .

Another novelty was the Latin. There had long been a smattering of Latin texts discovered in the buried villa. There was that intriguing fragment by Seneca the Elder just coming to light and half of a comic play by Caecilius Statius. And other tantalizing scraps. But they were few and far between and in terrible condition: in papyrological parlance, *non intero, poco leggibile, cattivo* (incomplete, barely legible, in bad shape).

The Caesar scroll suggested that there might be far more Latin documents to be discovered underground. Much as Brill valued Philodemus — Zeus knows, he'd spent vast amounts of time with him! — there was clearly more in the buried library of Herculaneum. More likely than not a separate Latin library as well as a Greek one. Imagine the possibilities! Aside from Sappho or Pythagoras, could Livy or Lucretius be among the scroll survivors?

And all those scrolls stashed away in the gunmetal cabinets, scrolls which stubbornly resisted physical unrolling: their moments of truth would also come, thanks to the new technology.

The letter from Caesar, to be sure, was a blockbuster. The media bonanza, the international headlines — he knew what to expect.

Brill felt fortunate that the Carabinieri for heritage art theft, in conjunction with the Officina, had consigned the scroll to him for editing. The pressure for the text to go to a local scholar was intense, naturally. So he was doing the work with an Italian colleague. That was fine, more than fine. He personally had no need for more academic hosannas. The intellectual stimulation, however, that he could always use. This was *ataraxia* distilled to a fine essence. Or virtual *ataraxia*.

Truth be told, he preferred working with the physical scrolls. Smelling, viewing, touching the papyri. Though actual touching was awkward given the uncomfortable nitrile gloves that were part of the new protocol.

"Can I help with anything, professor?"

"Thank you, Christoph, I will have some passages later that you can double-check the punctuation for."

"Of course."

The German papyrologist went back to his microscope. The police were not allowing any newcomers into the Officina until the criminal cases were settled. Brill could live with that. There were few interruptions. However, this period of enforced calm and monopoly over the texts wouldn't last forever. And reports in the sensational Italian media that a deadly curse hung over the papyri would eventually be laughed off, material for another witticism shared among scholars.

Meanwhile, there were many nuggets to dig up in the Caesar scroll, which more accurately was the Piso scroll, belonging to Lucius Calpurnius Piso Caesoninus, in all likelihood compiled by his son, Lucius Calpurnius Piso Frugi Pontifex, who inherited the Villa of the Papiri. A bust of Pontifex occupied pride of place in the Villa, surviving the volcano. The scroll contained his well-connected father's correspondence, which included that startling letter from Julius Caesar. But there was more, including another letter suggesting that, contrary to previous reports and chronicles, a young Egyptian prince had escaped the Roman conquest and had been living incognito in India.

A prince named Caesarion.

44

ATARAXIA

She watched him emerge from the police station, ducking under the traffic barrier framed by grey columns. A dreary building, Kristi thought, the sort of place where only bad news is delivered. She'd been watching the building all morning from a dingy café across the street. Why couldn't his hearing at the Corte d'Assise have been held in the Questura, that gleaming white police headquarters suggesting transparency and balance? Or the old courthouse on Via dei Tribunali, a baroque building radiating divine providence?

Yet his body language was good. She could read him now; five months cooped up with him during his house arrest had ensured that. And when Marcus crossed Via Medina, she noticed the absence of the tracking bracelet on his left hand.

"You're a free man!"

The passport in his right hand pressed against her back as they hugged with an intensity that capped all they'd been through these past months. Her rescue by police at the top of Vesuvius. The ten days of detention for Marcus. And afterwards, the antsy waiting with him under protracted house arrest in their Airbnb. Would the country's byzantine criminal justice system ensnare him? Would the conspiracy theories being peddled in the media — "Murder for Ancient Papyrus"; "Love Triangle Gone Wrong" — gain traction in court?

He was guilty, no doubt about it, of breaking and entering Sweeney's home; guilty of pointing a loaded weapon at the old man. It was not the smartest item on his curriculum vitae, and he'd spent no small amount of time anguishing over what reckless part of his psyche, what perfect storm of subatomic causation, led him to do those things. His trial produced guilty verdicts on both counts, and today's sentencing had been in the hands of the same judge who'd presided over the hearing. It was the best-case scenario they'd hoped for.

"Time served," Marcus said.

"Thank God! You were in there for ages. What happened?"

"The Italian justice system, that's what happened. I warned you. Have you been out here the whole time?"

"Fill me in."

"The judge laid out the basic facts. Time served under house arrest was sufficient for the breaking and entering, and the concealed weapon. She agreed to withdraw the attempted manslaughter charge. Gave me brownie points for formally relinquishing the scroll. They also set a date for Lorenzo's trial, next year. But the prosecutors seem certain that he killed Ballard with fentanyl."

"Fentanyl? Jesus! How the hell did that happen?"

"I have a knot in my stomach just thinking about it," Marcus said. "After having lunch at Festa, Lorenzo went to the hotel with Ballard to have the scroll authenticated. And somehow, he poisoned Ballard with fentanyl powder. Apparently, the powder was inside a pair of nitrile gloves he gave Ballard in order to handle the scroll. The police found traces of the same compound at Lorenzo's apartment, and also a box of those same white nitrile gloves, the kind the archivists use."

"But does fentanyl powder penetrate the skin in such a deadly way?"

"Not exactly. Once it was on Ballard's fingers, he would have had to rub his eyes or touched his ears or mouth to be killed by it."

She said, "I can't believe I'm hearing this."

Kristi had a flashback, one of many recently, this one to the time at the Officina when she'd first met Lorenzo and Christoph. How both of them waxed eloquent about that poem found in one papyrus, in which Cleopatra tested various types of poisons on prisoners so as to decide which one she'd use to kill herself. Lorenzo, or maybe Christoph, had declared it a thing of beauty.

She said, "What about Sweeney?"

"His statements to police were read in court. Sweeney purchased the scroll from Lorenzo. Legally, if you can believe that. There's apparently no evidence that he knew where or how Lorenzo obtained it."

"Not very believable," Kristi said.

"Agreed. And guess what he paid for it? Two hundred thousand dollars."

"What? How could Sweeney *not* want to know the provenance when paying that much?"

"Maybe he was happy not knowing too much. The lawyer's assistant was translating *sotto voce* for me in real time and I might have missed something. We'll have to read the transcript."

"That amount of money would have gone a long way in giving Lorenzo security. He hasn't finished his Ph.D. And job prospects for him were dismal. He was ranting about all this before the police showed up."

Lorenzo had panicked when he finally saw the Carabinieri approaching the summit; he scurried around trying to locate an alternative path down, but there was no way he was going to elude police at the top of the volcano. They arrested him in short order, finding a prohibited knife in his knapsack.

Marcus said, "I'm more than a little tempted to come back here for his trial."

They were arm in arm as they walked, cutting through the central core of the city.

"What else?"

"The judge grilled me forever about who gave me the gun and why. Gramsci is still a mystery man to them."

They made it to the section of the waterfront lined with seaside hotels and filled with joggers, cyclists, kite flyers, rollerbladers, and young couples canoodling on the sea wall. The outcropping on the coast a few feet below the road was occupied with sun-worshippers, their beach towels spread like giant postage stamps on the big flat rocks.

"When did you realize you were free?"

"I didn't. Not until the very end."

She wrapped herself around one of his arms as if for extra security — for him, not her. *Ciao*s here and there from passersby who recognized them from the media coverage; high-fives, handshakes, selfies even, which they did their best to decline.

"They don't seem to know where the Caesar scroll came from originally. I mean, they know Gerald got it somehow."

"Right. More material for me to dig into."

There would be time to gather all the details. Kristi's investigative piece had long ago spun out of control for newspaper length; she was contemplating a book.

Marcus gazed at the Castel Nuovo in the distance, a muscular fortification on the water's edge complete with moat and five imposing towers. It might have been a creation of Disney World had it not been a thousand years old. The fortress brought to mind a line from an ancient text.

"I'm thinking about something from Philodemus," he said. "His book, *On Death*."

"He'd have made a lousy headline writer."

"That's how books were titled way back when. *On Moral Duties. On Friendship. On Old Age. On Music.* On and on. Philodemus writes that we're born anew every day. That we have to live in the moment as a way of dealing with mortality."

"News flash," Kristi said. "Stop the press."

"Well, what's original at this point in time? And maybe clichés are clichés for a reason. Because they've earned their keep, having been seen and heard a zillion times every day in every country over the centuries."

Marcus went on: "He makes it sound more poetic than that. It's nothing like his usual polemics. More like his love poetry. It's an ode to life. Remember the Epicurean motto *we all live in a city without walls*? That was mortality for him."

"Walls?" Kristi said. "They should put up a wall around that crater on Vesuvius. I'm surprised kids on school outings don't tumble over."

"We've had enough souls plunging into Hades," he said. "Ballard. Sweeney, very nearly. You, almost."

"And you," she said, drawing him closer. "Anyway, Ingrid Bergman made the same point as Philodemus. With a shorter word count."

"Ingrid Bergman?"

"That old movie we watched, *Journey to Italy*? After Bergman and George Sanders view the plaster cast of a couple who died in the Vesuvius eruption, Bergman runs away and ends up on some ruins. She's shaken, crying. Sanders asks her what's the matter. 'Life is so short,' she says. 'That's why we should make the most of it.'"

"Philodemus's lover, Xanthippe, told him much the same thing," Marcus said. "It's in one of the poems. And it was less of a cliché back then."

They walked a bit more, propelled by some law of tourist gravity, up toward the Caffè Gambrinus.

"Remember," Marcus said, "I told you about a carnation farmer in Ercolano who contacted me? I didn't want to go into all the details until after the court hearing. Turns out he knew Gerald. I don't know how, exactly. He claims to have several scrolls that he dug up from old tunnels running under his farm, which led to the Villa. I figure it's worth checking out."

She said nothing, leading him to a stone wall at the edge of the piazza to contemplate the shimmering Bay of Naples.

He tried to envision the waterfront in the time of Philodemus. He subtracted the hotels, the selfie-sticks, the Vespas, everything less than two thousand years old. What remained was only the curvature of the coast, the sun, water, sky, the islands, the balmy air, and Vesuvius.

EPILOGUE

Instrumental music, stately and crisp, was filling the National Archaeological Museum. It was 1994, and Naples was a rougher place. The Camorra. The garbage. Purse-snatching. An earthquake and even a cholera outbreak. A third-world city, went the critique, with third-world politics.

Yet the mood had recently brightened. Naples was brimming with pride over its local soccer team, led by Maradona, which twice won the Italian football premiership. Andy Warhol's portraits of Vesuvius had been put on local exhibit. The G7 nations held their annual meeting in the city.

In this newfound spirit of civic pride, the National Archaeological Museum was the scene of a nighttime music festival. Normally at such a late hour, the museum doors were closed to the public. Poseidon, Athena, and the Farnese Bull would be enveloped in dead silence. The statues had to make do with the occasional crackle of a walkie-talkie and the echoing footsteps of night watchmen.

But on this evening, a Baroque music festival was underway.

For the museum to throw open its doors after hours and allow patrons to meander through galleries was a rare spectacle. In one cavernous room filled with art from Pompeii and Herculaneum, a chamber ensemble was performing Vivaldi — a dreamy combination of sights and sounds. The walls were hung with mosaics including that stunning picture of marine life in the Bay of Naples. The attendees, Naples high society for the most part, were justifiably enthralled.

As the Concerto in G Minor got underway, one man slipped out of the room, opening the heavy oak door and then closing it quietly behind him. Across the hallway, framed by columns, was another heavy door, which he opened. He entered, shutting the door behind him and wincing as it emitted a conspicuous squeak.

Moonlight through a tall, narrow window suffused an adjacent chamber; in that room he stopped before a large wooden apparatus that resembled a winepress. The intruder took a screwdriver from his satchel. He removed eight screws from a large plate of glass on the side of the machine. Two more screws were loosened inside the machine, and a blackened papyrus was gingerly removed. A black lump of similar cylindrical shape was taken from a small plastic box the man had also brought with him. The two objects swapped places.

One was a fake, made of papier-mâché. The authentic papyrus was placed in the plastic box and stashed in the man's satchel.

As the man replaced the glass and hurriedly tightened the screws, the tool slipped and cut the heel of his hand, drawing a thread of blood. He rolled up his sleeve to avoid getting it stained, revealing a tattoo on his forearm, a throwback to university days, a rose entwined with the letters PCI. The symbol of the Communist Party of Italy was not something he cared to flaunt anymore, especially in these surroundings. The trickle of blood was covered with a handkerchief tightened around his hand.

One last check of the Piaggio machine. And a glance over his shoulder at the painting of a mischievous cherub against a backdrop of Pompeian red.

"*Non hai visto niente*," he whispered to the cherub. *You saw nothing.* He made it back into the salon for the Bononcini sonata, handkerchief wrapped around his hand. His thoughts drifted to the man waiting for him at the Excelsior Hotel on the waterfront, the foreigner, Geraldo Sinclair.

ACKNOWLEDGEMENTS

The Fatal Scroll is a work of fiction inspired by the true story of Herculaneum. While the characters and plot are imaginary, much of the background and details are based on fact. For that, I am indebted to many papyrologists and experts, including Gianluca Del Mastro, Holger Essler, Kilian Fleischer, David Sider, Richard Janko, Daniel Delattre, Sanne Christensen, and John Stix. I am also grateful to Robert Fowler and Krystyna Cech of the Oxford-based Friends of Herculaneum Society. David Sutton, a scholar of Latin and Roman history, crafted most of the Latin fragment unrolled from "Gerald's scroll" and corrected some of my speculations about ancient history. Hannes Hoffmann, a keen observer of Herculaneum in its many layers, fact-checked an early version of the manuscript. Sean Johnson, a runner-up in the 2023 Vesuvius Challenge, explained the AI methods currently being used to distinguish carbon-based ink from carbonized papyrus. To all these experts, I give thanks; any errors or misinterpretations that remain in the book are solely the responsibility of the author.

I have drawn on the works of many scholars. In particular, I would like to acknowledge the following: David Sider, *The Library of the Villa dei Papiri at Herculaneum*; Tim O'Keefe, *Epicureanism*; Richard Janko, editor and translator with introduction and commentary of *On Poems, Book One*, by Philodemus; Gordon L. Fain, *Ancient Greek Epigrams: Major Poets in Verse Translation*; Carol C. Mattusch, *The Villa dei Papiri at Herculaneum: Life and Afterlife of a Sculpture Collection*; Marcello Gigante, *Philodemus in Italy: The Books from Herculaneum* (translated by Dirk Obbink); E.G. Turner, *Greek Papyri: An Introduction*; Roger S. Bagnall (ed.), *The Oxford Handbook of Papyrology*; John M. Cooper, *Pursuits of Wisdom: Six Ways of Life in Ancient Philosophy from Socrates to Plotinus*; Pierre Hadot, *What Is Ancient Philosophy?* (translated by Michael Chase).

This book would not have materialized without the feedback of many friends and editors. Daniel Sanger, Joel Simon, Josh Freed, Morey Richman, Adrienne Kerr, and especially Mike Levine, Mark Abley, and Susan Glickman greatly helped me improve this scroll as it unrolled. I'm very grateful to copy editor Peter Norman, who scrutinized everything from *sfogliatella* to Xanthippe and provided invaluable suggestions. He also restructured the translations of Philodemus's epigrams. I thank Jack David, Samantha Chin, and everyone else at ECW Press who helped transform a manuscript into a published book. Thanks as well to James Taylor for creating the book's website at thefatalscroll.com.

The translations of three epigrams by Philodemus in chapters 10 and 31 are slight variations on those found at attalus.org, which are in turn based on *The Greek Anthology*, vol. one, translated by W.R. Paton, 1927 edition, originally published in 1916 by W. Heinemann (London) and G.P. Putnam's Sons (New York).

The Greek text in chapter 7 is a truncated version of another epigram by Philodemus when he invites Piso to a dinner to celebrate the birthday of Epicurus (January 20). It is also based on the W.R. Paton translation, which can be found at attalus.org. I interpolated dashes to suggest lacunae in a damaged, carbonized papyrus roll. The full epigram in English reads as follows:

Tomorrow, dearest Piso, your friend, beloved by the Muses, who keeps our annual feast of the twentieth, invites you to come after the ninth hour to his simple cottage. If you miss udders and draughts of Chian wine, you will see at least sincere friends, and you will hear things far sweeter than the land of Phaeacians. But if you ever cast your eyes on me, Piso, we shall celebrate the twentieth richly instead of simply.

The Epicurean epigraph that begins this book is taken from *Letters, Principal Doctrines, and Vatican Sayings* by Epicurus, translated by Russel M. Geer.

Finally, thanks to my mother, Jacqueline Siblin, for giving me a copy of *The Economist*, in which I read a line that went something like: "Multi-spectral imaging has been used to help decipher the carbonized papyrus scrolls at Herculaneum." I had no idea what the sentence meant, and it piqued my curiosity.

Entertainment. Writing. Culture. ─────────

ECW is a proudly independent, Canadian-owned book publisher. We know great writing can improve people's lives, and we're passionate about sharing original, exciting, and insightful writing across genres.

───────────────────── **Thanks for reading along!**

We want our books not just to sustain our imaginations, but to help construct a healthier, more just world, and so we've become a certified B Corporation, meaning we meet a high standard of social and environmental responsibility — and we're going to keep aiming higher. We believe books can drive change, but the way we make them can too.

Certified

Corporation

Being a B Corp means that the act of publishing this book should be a force for good — for the planet, for our communities, and for the people that worked to make this book. For example, everyone who worked on this book was paid at least a living wage. You can learn more at the Ontario Living Wage Network.

This book is also available as a Global Certified Accessible™ (GCA) ebook. ECW Press's ebooks are screen reader friendly and are built to meet the needs of those who are unable to read standard print due to blindness, low vision, dyslexia, or a physical disability.

This book is printed on FSC®-certified paper. It contains recycled materials, and other controlled sources, is processed chlorine free, and is manufactured using biogas energy.

FSC
www.fsc.org

MIX
Paper | Supporting
responsible forestry
FSC® C103567

ECW's office is situated on land that was the traditional territory of many nations, including the Wendat, the Anishinaabeg, Haudenosaunee, Chippewa, Métis, and current treaty holders the Mississaugas of the Credit. In the 1880s, the land was developed as part of a growing community around St. Matthew's Anglican and other churches. Starting in the 1950s, our neighbourhood was transformed by immigrants fleeing the Vietnam War and Chinese Canadians dispossessed by the building of Nathan Phillips Square and the subsequent rise in real estate value in other Chinatowns. We are grateful to those who cared for the land before us and are proud to be working amidst this mix of cultures.

ecwpress.com